My Tall Green Friends

Ruskin Bond is known for his signature simplistic and witty writing style. He is the author of several bestselling short stories, novellas, collections, essays and children's books; and has contributed a number of poems and articles to various magazines and anthologies. At the age of twenty-three, he won the prestigious John Llewellyn Rhys Prize for his first novel, *The Room on the Roof*. He was also the recipient of the Padma Shri in 1999, Lifetime Achievement Award by the Delhi Government in 2012, and the Padma Bhushan in 2014.

Born in 1934, Ruskin Bond grew up in Jamnagar, Shimla, New Delhi and Dehradun. Apart from three years in the UK, he has spent all his life in India, and now lives in Landour, Mussoorie, with his adopted family.

RUSKIN
BOND

My Tall Green Friends

RUPA

Published by
Rupa Publications India Pvt. Ltd 2018
7/16, Ansari Road, Daryaganj
New Delhi 110002

Sales centres:
Allahabad Bengaluru Chennai
Hyderabad Jaipur Kathmandu
Kolkata Mumbai

ISBN: 978-93-5304-605-7

First impression 2018

10 9 8 7 6 5 4 3 2 1

CONTENTS

INTRODUCTION

Trees make for great friends. They are sturdy and dependable; can listen to you for hours while you pour your heart out; they do not complain if you pluck their fruits or flowers; are always ready to provide you shade or a place to rest under. Fortunately for me, there are plenty of such friends to be made in the mountains and plains of India. I can never run out of them or have enough of them.

With the company of the great trees, come the birds, the squirrels, the monkeys and langurs, and the insects. All making for enjoyable companions, but not from too close.

In my childhood and youth, I have climbed all sorts of trees—from the jackfruit tree to the guava and litchi trees, from the large oaks to the very difficult cedars. I've climbed the lot and I've got scars to this day to prove it.

The pace may be slower here in the mountains, but there is no dearth of the stories that one can unearth. For instance, look at my numerous visitors from the forests. There was once a bat who had adopted, what seemed to me, an odd style of flying. Like a dive bomber it flew into my room after dark, looking for tasty moths to snap up. I wondered what was wrong with it, till I found that this indeed was a kind of bat that had been written about earlier—much earlier, in 1884. It pleased me that something that was rare even then had chosen to present itself in my home. Other times, I've had squirrels and praying mantis and birds of various kinds sit at the window or sometimes drop in, take a look and then go their way. We take a good close look at each other when we meet, and I flatter myself to think that perhaps they like what they see—as much as I like having these little guests.

Over these years I have also traipsed a fair bit around these hills and mountains, exploring forests and foothills and hamlets. Some journeys have been to the holy places that dot the high reaches—Kedarnath, Badrinath, Gangotri, etc. Here, the sight of the old temples and the high majestic peaks remain etched in the mind long after one has returned home. The moment, in Badrinath, when I opened my eyes one morning and looked out of the window to see the magnificent Nilkantha peak bathed in the light of the rising sun is as astonishing and spectacular in my mind's eye even now.

With the twenty-two stories that I have put together here, I intend to introduce you to my friends in these Himalayas— from the animals and insects that visit me to the tall trees I visit regularly; they'd all like to say hello to you and tell you all about our meetings.

Ruskin Bond

WHITE CLOUDS, GREEN MOUNTAINS

Towards the end of September, those few monsoon clouds that still linger over the Himalayas are no longer burdened with rain and are able to assume unusual shapes and patterns, chasing each other across the sky and disappearing in spectacular sunset formations.

I have always found this to be the best time of the year in the hills. The sun-drenched hillsides are still an emerald green; the air is crisp, but winter's bite is still a month or two away; and for those who still like to take to the open road on foot, there are springs, streams and waterfalls tumbling over rocks that remain dry for most of the year. The lizard that basked on a sun-baked slab of granite last May is missing, but in his place the spotted forktail trips daintily among the boulders in a stream; and the strident sound of the cicadas is gradually replaced by the gentler trilling of the crickets and grasshoppers.

Cicadas, as you probably know, make their music with their legs, which are moved like the bows of violins against their bodies. It's rather like an orchestra tuning up but never quite getting on with the overture or symphony. Aunt Ruby, who is a little deaf, can nevertheless hear the cicadas when they are at their loudest. She lives not far from a large boarding school, and one day when I remarked that I could hear the school choir or choral group singing, she nodded and remarked: 'Yes, dear. They do it with their legs, don't they?'

Come to think of it, that school choir does sound a bit squeaky.

Now, more than at any other time of the year, the wildflowers come into their own.

The hillside is covered with a sward of flowers and ferns. Sprays of wild ginger, tangles of clematis, flat clusters of yarrow and lady's mantle. The datura grows everywhere with its graceful white balls and prickly fruits. And the wild woodbine provides the stems from which the village boys make their flutes.

Aroids are plentiful and attract attention by their resemblance to snakes with protruding tongues—hence the popular name, cobra lily. This serpent's tongue is a perfect landing-stage for flies etc., who, crawling over the male flowers in their eager search for the liquor that lies at the base of the spike (a liquor that is most appealing to their depraved appetites), succeed in fertilizing the female flowers as they proceed. We see that it is not only humans who become addicted to alcohol. Bears have been known to get drunk on the juice of rhododendron flowers, while bumble bees can be out-and-out dipsomaniacs.

One of the more spectacular cobra lilies, which rejoices in the name *Sauromotum Guttatum*—ask your nearest botanist what that means!—bears a solitary leaf and purple spathe. When the seeds form, it withdraws the spike underground; and when the rains are over and the soil is not too damp, it sends it up again covered with scarlet berries. In the opinion of the hill folk, the appearance of the red spike is more to be relied on as a forecast of the end of the monsoon than any meteorological expertise. Up here on the ranges that fall between the Jumna and the Bhagirathi (known as the Rawain), we can be perfectly sure of fine weather a fortnight after the fiery spike appears.

But it is the commelina, more than any other Himalayan flower, that takes my breath away. The secret is in its colour—a pure pristine blue that seems to reflect the deepest blue of the sky. Towards the end of the rains it appears as if from nowhere, graces the hillside for the space of about two weeks, and disappears again until the following monsoon.

When I see the first commelina, I stand dumb before it and the world stands still while I worship. So absorbed do I become in its delicate beauty that I begin to doubt the reality of everything else in the world.

But only for a moment. The blare of a truck's horn reminds me that I am still lingering on the main road leading out of the hill station. A cloud of dust and blasts of diesel fumes are further indications that reality takes many different forms, assailing all my senses at once! Even my commelina seems to shrink from the onslaught. But as it is still there, I take heart and leave the highway for a lesser road.

Soon I have left the clutter of the town behind. What did Aunt Ruby say the other day? 'Stand still for five minutes, and they will build a hotel on top of you.'

Wasn't it Lot's wife who was turned into a pillar of salt when she looked back at the doomed city that had been her home? I have an uneasy feeling that I will be turned into a pillar of cement if I look back, so I plod on along the road to Devsari, a kindly village in the valley. It will be some time before 'developers' and big money boys get here, for no one will go to live where there is no driveway!

A tea-shop beckons. How would one manage in the hills without these wayside tea-shops? Miniature inns, they provide food, shelter, and even lodging to dozens at a time.

I tackle some buns that have a pre-Independence look about them. They are rock-hard, to match the environment, but I manage to swallow some of the jagged pieces with the hot sweet tea, which is good.

THE WONDERFUL WORLD OF INSECTS

When you have some time to spare, make a list of all the different insects that you can name. If you can put more than twenty names on your list, you will probably do better than the average person. But suppose you knew the name of every kind of insect in India or even in the world. If you were to write them all down, it would take you at least a month, without stopping to sleep or eat, to complete your list. There are over a million species, with thousands more being discovered each year.

When you have made your list, look it over carefully, for it is quite possible that you have included some animals that are not insects at all. Scorpions, spiders, and mites are often mistaken for insects, but—though I have included them in this book—they belong to another group of small animals. If you know what to look for, it is quite easy to tell whether or not an animal is an insect.

A moth, a honeybee, and a mosquito do not look very much alike, yet each is an insect. If you examine them, you will find certain similarities. Each one of these animals has six legs, as all insects have, with a body divided into three parts: a head, a centre part, and an abdomen. If you remember these two characteristics, you will be able to recognize an insect. The next time you look at a spider, you will see that it has not six but eight legs, and its body only two parts instead of three. For this reason it is not called an insect.

The skeleton of an insect is external, and the muscles and nerves inside are not only protected by this outer covering but combine with it to make the creature surprisingly strong and durable. For example, a beetle can support, without collapsing, some eight hundred times its own weight!

Insects are found almost everywhere—from steaming jungles to polar regions, in the soil, in the air and in the water. They seem to be able to live and thrive under almost any conditions. They have no lungs but breathe through air ducts in the sides of the body, the air being circulated to all parts through an intricate system of tiny tubes.

In beauty and colour some insects have no equal in the animal world, while structurally each one is a miracle.

The compound eyes of an insect are composed of many units or separate eyes, each of which transmits an image of what is seen to the brain. They enable the insect to detect the slightest movement of its enemy or prey.

The number of eye-units vary with different insects. The silver fish has 12, some ants have 50, cockroaches 1,800, houseflies 4,000, butterflies 17,000, and dragonflies from 20,000 to 30,000. In addition to the compound eyes, most insects have simple eyes—usually three placed on top of the forehead—which only distinguish between light and dark. Some beetles have two simple eyes placed on the back of the head.

The energy of an insect is tremendous. A flea can jump over one hundred times its height. A mosquito in flight has a wing-beat of three hundred per second. A dragonfly can attain a speed of nearly sixty miles an hour. The Painted Lady butterfly makes a migratory trip from North Africa to as far as Iceland.

Anyone who has stepped on a cockroach, been bitten by a mosquito or bothered by flies, will tell you that some insects are a nuisance. They not only interfere with our activities at times, but they also do damage to the extent of crores of rupees each year in our country alone. Most of the damage is done by insects that feed on plants that we use, insects such as the cotton-destroying boll weevil, the potato beetle and the tobacco hornworm. Also, some kinds of insects—especially flies—carry diseases, and we try to control them on this account.

But not all insects are harmful.

If all insects were to suddenly disappear from the earth, it would not be long before many other living things would vanish too, possibly even mankind.

Many vegetables and flowering plants would die, for these plants cannot bear fruit or seeds unless an insect transfers their pollen. Fishes and birds that feed on insects would vanish, and many of the animals that depend, in turn, on these fishes and birds for food would soon starve.

Once a link in nature's chain of life is broken or removed, the entire chain is in danger of falling apart.

THE GALLERY OF BIRDS

Having divided the last many years of my life between Delhi and Mussoorie, I have come to the heretical conclusion that there is more bird life in cities than there in the hills and forests around our hill stations. For birds to survive, they have to learn to live with and upon humans and those birds like crows, sparrows and mynahs who do this to perfection, continue to thrive as our cities grow, whereas the purely wild birds, those who depend upon the forests for life, are rapidly disappearing, simply because the forests are disappearing.

Recently, I saw more birds in one week in a New Delhi colony than I had seen during a month in the hills. In the hills, one must be patient and alert if one is to spot just a few of the birds so beautifully described in Salim Ali's *Indian Hill Birds*. The babblers and thrushes are still around but the fly-catchers and warblers are seldom seen or heard.

But in Delhi, if you have just a bit of garden and perhaps a guava tree, you will be visited by innumerable bulbuls, tailor birds mynahs, hoopoes, parrots, and tree-pies. Or if you own an old house you will have to share it with pigeons and sparrows, perhaps swallows or swifts. And if you have neither a garden nor a rooftop, you will be visited by crows.

Wherever man goes, the crow follows. He has learnt to perfect the art of living off humans. He will, I am sure, be the first bird on the moon, scavenging among the paper bags and cartons left behind by untidy astronauts.

Crows favour the densest areas of human population and there must be at least one for every human. Many crows have obviously been humans in previous lives; they are as cunning and possess the sense of self-preservation of the human being. At the same time, there are many humans who have obviously been crows and haven't lost their thieving instincts.

Watch a crow sidling along a garden wall with a shabby genteel air, cocking a speculative eye at the kitchen door and any attendant humans. He reminds me of a newspaper reporter hovering in the background until his chance comes— then pouncing! I have even known a crow to make off with an egg from the breakfast table. No other bird except perhaps the sparrow has been so successful in exploiting human beings.

The mynah, although he too is quite at home in the city, is more of a gentleman. He prefers fruit on the tree to scraps from the kitchen, and visits the garden much out of a sense of sociability as in expectation of hand-outs. He is quite handsome too, with his bright orange bill and the mask around his eyes. He is equally at home on a railway platform as on the ear of a grazing buffalo, and, being omnivorous, has no trouble in co-existing with man.

The sparrow on the other hand is not a gentleman. Uninvited, he enters your home, followed by his friends, relatives and political hangers-on, and proceeds to quarrel and leave his droppings on the sofa cushions with a complete disregard for the presence of humans. The party will then proceed towards the garden and destroy all the flower buds. No birds have succeeded so well in making fools out of humans.

Although the blue jay (or roller) is quite capable of making his living in the forest, he seems to show a preference for the haunts of men and would rather perch on a telegraph wire than in a tree. Probably, he finds the wire a better launching pad for his sudden rocket flights and aerial acrobatics. In repose, he is rather shabby but in flight when his outspread wings reveal his brilliant blues, he takes one's breath away. His food consists of beetles and other insects and pests, he can be considered a friend and an ally.

Parrots make little or no distinction between town and country life. They are the freelancers of the bird world—sturdy, independent, and noisy. With flashes of blue and green, they swoop across the road, settle for a while in a mango tree and then with shrill, delighted cries, move on to some other field or orchard. They will sample all the food they can without finishing any. They are destructive birds but because of their bright plumage, graceful flight and charming ways, are popular favourites and can get away with anything. No one who has enjoyed watching a flock of parrots in carefree flight would want to cage one of these virile birds. Yet many people do cage them.

After the peacock, perhaps the most popular bird in rural India is the sarus crane—a familiar sight around jheels and river banks of northern India and Gujarat. The sarus pairs for life and is seldom seen without its mate. When one bird dies, the other often pines away and seemingly dies of grief. It is this near human quality of devotion that has earned the birds this popularity with the villagers of the plains. As a result they are well-protected.

In the long run, it is the 'common man' and not the scientist or conservationist who can best give protection to the birds and animals living around him. Religious sentiment has helped preserve the peacock and a few other birds. It is a pity that other equally beautiful birds do not enjoy the same protection.

But the wily crow, the cheeky sparrow and the sensible mynah will always be with us. Quite possibly they will survive even longer than the human species. And it is the same with other animals. While the cringing jackal has learnt the art of survival, his master, the magnificent tiger is on its way to extinction.

SOUNDS OF THE SEA

For years I had this large seashell, and by putting it to my ear I could hear the distant sob and hiss of the sea—or so I fancied, until this romantic notion was dispelled by twelve-year-old Mukesh, who told me that the same effect could be obtained by holding an empty cup to my ear. He was right, of course. In fact, the cup sounds better than the shell! And for years I'd gone on imagining that the sound of the sea was somehow trapped in my shell... But I still cling to it, for it takes me back to Jamnagar, on the west coast of India, and memories of sea and sand, small steamers and large Arab dhows plying across the Gulf of Kutch.

My small hand in my father's, I explored with him the little port's harbour and beach, bringing home shells of considerable variety, and even, on one occasion, a small crab, which lived in a spare bathtub for several days and was forgotten—until a visiting aunt, deciding on a tub-bath after a long train journey, found it keeping her company among the soap-suds. Amidst much clamour and consternation, it was evicted from the house and dropped into a nearby well. But my aunt was convinced that I had deliberately placed it in the tub, and refused to speak to me for the rest of her stay.

A small British steamer was often in port, and my father and I would visit the captain, a good-natured Welshman who gave me chocolates, a great treat in those days, for Jamnagar was too small a place for a Western confectionery shop. I was ready to go to sea with Captain Jenkins, convinced that chocolates were only to be found on tramp steamers.

We left Jamnagar when the Second World War broke out and my father joined the R.A.F. It was to be some ten years before I saw the sea again, for I went to boarding school in the hills. I was still in my teens, but now bereft of my father, when I set sail from Bombay in the *S.S. Strathnaver*, a beautiful P&O liner, one of a fleet, its sister ships being the *Strathaird* and *Stratheden*. Those were the days of the big passenger liners, before fast air travel put an end to leisurely ocean voyages. It took just over a fortnight to reach Southampton or London, but there was never a dull moment on the voyage. Apart from interesting shipboard acquaintances—the sort of mixed company that gave Somerset Maugham material for his stories—there were also colourful ports of call: Aden, Port Said, Marseilles, Gibraltar, etc. At Marseilles, I decided to miss the coach-tour and instead walk into the town. After three hours of walking along miles and miles of dockland, I finally reached the outskirts of the city—just in time to catch the coach back to the ship!

But later, living in London, I never tired of walking among the docks and wharfs along the Thames, for many of those places were associated with the novels of Dickens, which had inspired me to become a writer. Limehouse, Wapping, Shadwell Stairs, the Mile End Road, the East India Docks, these were all places I knew from *Bleak House*, *Dumbey and Son*, and *Our Mutual Friend*. And there was the fog, a thick pea souper, that seemed to have lingered on from the fog that had enveloped the characters and the action in *Bleak House*, setting the tone for that masterpiece. London, I am told, no longer has fogs—they are dispersed by modern and scientific means—and although the air no doubt is cleaner and healthier now, I feel sure some of the magic has gone—along with the East End of old.

From London's dockland to the Channel Islands was a short trip but a considerable change. I lived on the island of Jersey for two years. It had a number of bays and inlets of great charm and beauty, and it was here that I learnt to watch the tides advancing and retreating, and discovered that the tides make different sounds in different places.

Every tide has its own music, and those who live near lonely shores soon learn to recognize the familiar ripple, throb, sob, or sigh. And sometimes the tide comes up from the deep against a steep sand-bank and roars defiance.

The tide-rip which pushes through the Channel Islands off the Norman coast has a smoother thud than most, though it comes from the same Atlantic as the harsher-sounding waters among the Orkneys. The difference may be that the channel tides move through purple waters which have drifted up from sunny Portugal, while the other has a shiver from the coast of Greenland.

The music of sea waters is wonderfully varied. Every bay and headland and strait has its note which the local fisherfolk recognize even in time of dense fog; a note which guides them home or which helps them locate the place for their fishing.

For many years I have been living far from the sea. Sometimes I feel the urge to go down to the sea again, all the way from the Himalayas to Cape Comorin. And maybe I will one day.

Meanwhile, if I wish to listen to the sound of the sea, there's always my seashell—or Mukesh's tea-cup.

A MOUNTAIN STREAM

There is a brook at the bottom of the hill. From where I live I can always hear its murmur, but I am no longer conscious of the sound except when I return from a trip to the plains. And yet I have grown so used to the constant music of water that when I leave it behind I feel naked and alone, bereft of my moorings. It is like getting accustomed to the friendly rattle of tea cups every morning, and then waking one day to an empty stillness and a fleeting moment of panic.

Below the house is a forest of oak and maple and Himalayan rhododendron. A path twists its way down through the trees, over an open ridge where red sorrel grows wild, and then down steeply through a bangle of thorn bushes, creepers, and rangal bamboo. At the bottom of the hill the path leads on to a grassy verge, surrounded by wild roses. The stream runs close by the verge, tumbling over smooth pebbles, over rocks worn yellow with age, on its way to the plains and to the little Song river and finally to the sacred Ganges.

When I first discovered the stream it was April and the wild roses were flowering, small white blossoms lying in clusters. There were still pink and blue primroses on the hill-slopes, and an occasional late-flowering rhododendron provided a splash of crimson against the dark green of the hill.

A spotted forktail, a bird of the Himalayan streams was much in evidence during those early visits. It moved nimbly over the boulders with a fairy tread, and continually wagged its tail. Both of us had a fondness for standing in running water. Once, while I stood in the stream, I saw a snake swim past, a slim brown snake, beautiful and lonely. A snake in water is a lovely creature.

In May and June, when the hills were always brown and dry, it remained cool and green near the stream, where ferns and maidenhair and long grasses continued to thrive. Downstream I found a small pool where I could bathe, and a cave with water dripping from the roof, the water spangled gold and silver in the shafts of sunlight that pushed through the slits in the cave roof.

Few people came there. Sometimes a milkman or a coal-burner would cross the stream on his way to a village; but the nearby hill station's summer visitors had not discovered this haven of wild and green things.

The monkeys—langurs, with white and silver-grey fur, black faces and long swishing tails—had discovered the place, but they kept to the trees and sunlit slopes. They grew quite accustomed to my presence, and carried on about their work and play as though I did not exist. They were clean and polite, much nicer than the red monkeys of the plains.

During the rains the stream became a rushing torrent, bushes and small trees were swept away, and the friendly murmur of the water became a threatening boom. I did not visit the place too often, as there were leeches in the long grass. But it was always worthwhile tramping through the forest to feast my eyes on the foliage that sprang up in tropical profusion—soft, springy moss; great stag-ferns on the trunks of trees; mysterious and sometimes evil-looking lilies and orchids; wild dahlias, and the climbing convolvulus opening its purple secrets to the morning sun.

And when the rains were over and it was October and the birds were in song again, I could lie in the sun, on sweet-smelling grass, land gaze up through a pattern of oak leaves into a blinding-blue heaven. And I would thank my God for leaves and grass, and the smell of things—the smell of mint and myrtle and bruised clover, and the touch of things—the touch of grass and air and sky, the touch of the sky's blueness.

And then, after a November hailstorm, it was winter, and I could not lie on the frost yellowed grass. The sound of the stream was the same, but I missed the birds; and the grey skies came clutching at my heart, and the rain and sleet drove me indoors.

It snowed—the snow lay heavy on the branches of the oak trees and piled up in the culverts—and grass and the ferns and wildflowers were pressed to sleep beneath a cold white blanket; but the stream flowed on, pushing its way through and under the whiteness, towards another river, towards another spring.

THE CHARMING BLOODSUCKER

No, this article is not about the village moneylender, but about the garden lizard—a little creature who is found in almost every Indian garden and who has done nothing to deserve the name by which he is known.

How this lizard came by the name of bloodsucker is a mystery, because it certainly does not suck blood. This misnomer might have originated through a popular superstition in some parts of India. There are people who believe that this harmless lizard—its real name is Calotes versicolor—has the power of sucking a person's blood simply by looking at him. It is also believed that the lizard changes its colour to red because of the blood it has absorbed in this way!

Not Conspicous

Give a lizard a bad name and it's sure to stick. And so the harmless garden lizard, like the equally harmless gecko or wall lizard, has been credited with all the powers of darkness and is often cruelly put to death.

The bloodsucker (too late to change its name to anything

else) does of course change its colour to some degree under ordinary circumstances, although it is not as gifted as the chameleon in this respect; it reserves its most vivid colour changes for the breeding season. So if you see a garden lizard turning a bright red, this is not because it is absorbing your blood, but because it is in love—not with you, but with a female of its own species.

As a rule the bloodsucker is not conspicuous. This is not because it remains in hiding. It likes warmth and light, and may often be seen basking in the morning sun, on the alert for some unwary insect. Light brown or greyish, its colour easily blends with the varied hues of its surroundings, which is why it often goes unnoticed.

During the cold season, bloodsuckers seek shelter in hollow trunks or holes in the ground, or enter houses where they hide behind furniture and curtains. They emerge from these retreats only during the warmest time of the day, to sunbathe and indulge in a little exercise. During the summer months they spend nearly all their time in the open.

It is during the breeding season that they undergo a remarkable change of colour. While the female confines herself to a maidenly blush, the male dons the most gaudy attire, his head, shoulders, and a part of his forelegs becoming crimson or scarlet, while black patches appear on either side of the throat and on the shoulders.

The gorgeously painted male sits on a fence or the trunk of a tree, surveying the neighbourhood. His manners are as loud as his dress, and he is out to seek a quarrel. From time to time he will jerk his head and shoulders up and down, a challenge to all other males in the vicinity.

Like Warriors

Two males about to fight will first charge each other from a distance like warriors of old. On meeting, both stand on hind legs and fall, gripping each other with forelegs and trying to bite. Toes or a portion of the tail often get bitten off in such an encounter. However, even with lizards—as with professional wrestlers—there is a good deal of pretence and very often the fight stops as abruptly as it began, one of the lizards making a hasty retreat.

At the time of courtship a curious performance is put through by the male. He chooses a convenient spot, then advances cautiously towards the female. He is then a pale flesh-colour. He stands upright raising the forepart of the body as high as possible and solemnly nods his head up and down. As he does this, his mouth rapidly opens and closes a number of times. Then, as he closes upon the female, his colours grow more vivid. But after separating he is almost colourless again.

If the amorous male is driven away, caught, or killed, the dark spot disappears entirely from his neck; and as happens among almost all forms of life, another male takes his place within a few hours.

Apart from superstitious humans, the garden lizard's chief enemies are large birds such as crows or blue jays who are only too ready to make a meal of him. But the bloodsucker is an agile little creature and his long slender tail, which easily comes apart from the rest of his body, is also a great protection. It often happens that a bird seizes a lizard by the long tail. Then the lizard, by leaving its tail behind in the bird's beak, is able to escape with its life. The bird goes on killing the old tail, and the lizard begins growing a new one.

TREES OF THE HIMALAYAS

India is probably nowhere so rich in forests as in the Himalayas, where the hills and valleys provide so many contrasts in elevation, humidity and temperature that a great variety of vegetation is to be found all the year round.

Ascending the foothills, no very sudden change is noticed, and it almost seems that the vast stretch of forest lying in the still heat is merely a duplicate of the forest in the plains. But this is sal forest, which covers the foothills with speed and persistence. The more vigorous sal trees grow rapidly, the weaker bide their time until the death or destruction of their more powerful fellows.

A sal forest has a remarkably individual character, where, from tiny sapling to giant patriarch, each tree ruthlessly waits for the downfall of its neighbour: a restless, ambitious sea of foliage, some trees attaining a height of 150 feet and a girth of twenty feet.

The sal is the most important tree of the lower Himalayas, providing the bulk of railway sleepers in India and yielding, when tapped, a large quantity of good resin. The flowers, tiny and sweet-scented, appear in March, in some places heralding a spring festival, when baskets of them are carried from village to village and distributed to women as emblems of motherhood.

Beyond the sal forests, the hillside changes in appearance. The undergrowth is not so tall. It thins out, and the only features suggesting tropical vegetation are the giant mops of the screw pine and the beautiful tree ferns.

Now the birch and the poplar prevail. The Himalayan birches, growing singly, are more valued for their bark than for their timber. The bark is cast off in wide, horizontal shreds, and is exported far and wide for tanning, papermaking and lining of hookahs. The poplar's broad, heart-shaped leaves readily flutter to every breeze; and apart from the tree's ornamental value, its close-grained timber is used for beams and rafters.

In the eastern hills, where the monsoon is heavy, the atmosphere is too humid for the coniferous family, but just suits the immigrant Japanese cedar, which grows with such persistence that many of these trees, trim and beautiful and straight, are found at elevations of 4,000 to 6,000 feet—elevations which also happen to suit most of the flora of temperate Europe.

The oak and the chestnut grow profusely above 5,000 feet. The fruit of the chestnut is beloved by the Lepchas of Sikkim, and the wood of this tree provides the big pestles and mortars used for crashing millets, which are converted into local beer.

On the more exposed hills grow the maples, trees of no great size or thickness, but of striking appearance in the spring and autumn by the variety of crimson and gold tints in their foliage. There are several species of maple, and the best drinking cups in Tibet are made from the knobs of one particular kind of tree.

The walnut is a native of the eastern Himalayas, and bears a high percentage of good nuts. It is also in great demand for making furniture.

The rhododendrons and magnolias are the most admired trees of the Himalayas. The rhododendron's magnificent cluster of pink and crimson bells explains the meaning of its name—rhododendron, rose tree!

Near Darjeeling in West Bengal, the magnolia has deep wine-coloured flowers, which are very fragrant—so sweet that they have been known to cause giddiness to the inhaler.

The pine, deodar, cedar, yew, and spruce are all well-known conifers in the Himalayas. Many beautiful bamboos abound in the hills—one species is used by the Lepchas for making bows, another is used in floating heavy logs and a third, when cut, shortened and flattened out, serves the purpose of tiles; it is durable and watertight.

The peach and the apricot, the plum and the cherry, grow wild and in cultivation, and their delicate pink and white blossoms add charm and grace to the grandeur of the Himalayas.

MY TALL GREEN FRIENDS

Living for many years in a cottage at 7,000 feet in the Garhwal Himalayas, I was fortunate in having a big window that opened out on the forest, so that the trees were almost within my reach. Had I jumped, I should have landed safely in the arms of an oak or chestnut.

The incline of the hill was such that my first-floor window opened on what must, I suppose, have been the second floor. I never made the jump, but the big langurs, silver-red monkeys with long swishing tails, often leapt from the trees onto the corrugated tin roof and made enough noise to disturb the bats sleeping in the space between the roof and ceiling.

Standing on its own was a walnut tree, and truly, this was a tree for all seasons. In winter its branches were bare but they were smooth and straight and round like the arms of a woman in a painting by Jamini Roy. In the spring each branch produced a hard bright spear of new leaf. By mid-summer the entire tree was in leaf, and towards the end of the monsoon the walnuts, encased in their green jackets, had reached maturity.

Then the jackets began to split, revealing the hard black-shell of the walnuts. Inside the shell was the nut itself. Look closely at the nut and you will notice that it is shaped rather like the human brain. No wonder the ancients prescribed walnuts for headaches!

Every year the tree gave me a basket of walnuts. But last year the walnuts were disappearing one by one, and I was at a loss as to know who had been taking them. Could it have been Biju, the milkman's son? He was an inveterate tree climber. But he was usually to be found on oak trees, gathering fodder for his cows. He told me that his cows liked oak leaves but did not care for walnuts. He admitted that they had relished my dahlias, which they had eaten the previous week, but he denied having fed them walnuts.

It wasn't the woodpecker. He was out there everyday, knocking furiously against the bark of the tree, trying to prise an insect out of a narrow crack. He was strictly non-vegetarian and none the worse for it.

One day I found a fat langur sitting in the walnut tree. I watched him for some time to see if he was going to help himself to the nuts, but he was only sunning himself. When he thought I wasn't looking, he came down and ate the geraniums, but he did not take any walnuts.

The walnuts had been disappearing early in the morning while I was still in bed. So one morning I surprised everyone, including myself, by getting up before sunrise. I was just in time to catch the culprit climbing out of the walnut tree.

She was an old woman who sometimes came to cut grass on the hillside. Her face was as wrinkled as the walnuts she had been helping herself to. In spite of her age, her arms and legs were sturdy. When she saw me, she was as swift as a civet-cat in getting out of the tree.

'And how many walnuts did you gather today, grandmother?'

'Only two,' she said with a giggle, offering them to me on her open palm. I accepted one of them. Encouraged, she climbed back into the tree and helped herself to the remaining nuts. It was impossible to object. I was taken up in admiration of her agility in the tree. She must have been about sixty, and I was a mere forty-five, but I knew I would never be climbing trees again.

To the victor the spoils!

The horse-chestnuts are inedible, even the monkeys throw them away in disgust. Once, on passing beneath a horse-chestnut tree, a couple of chestnuts bounced off my head. Looking up, I saw that they had been dropped on me by a couple of mischievous rhesus monkeys.

The tree itself is a friendly one, especially in summer when it is in full leaf. The least breath of wind makes the leaves break into conversation and their rustle is a cheerful sound, unlike the sad notes of pine trees in the wind. The spring flowers look like candlebra, and when the blossoms fall they carpet the hillside with their pale pink petals.

We pass now to my favourite tree, the deodar. In Garhwal and Kumaon it is called 'dujar' or 'devdar', in Jaunsar and in parts of Himachal it is known as the 'kelu kelon'.

Trees, like humans, change with their environment. Several persons familiar with the deodar at Indian hill stations, when asked to point it out in London's Kew Gardens, indicated the cedar of Lebanon, and shown a deodar, declared they had never seen such a tree in the Himalayas!

We shall stick to the name deodar, which comes from the Sanskrit 'deva-daru' (divine tree). It is a sacred tree in the Himalayas; neither worshipped, nor protected in the way that a peepul is in the plains, but sacred in that its timber has always been used in temples for doors, windows, walls, and even roofs. Quite frankly, I would just as soon worship the deodar as worship anything, for in its beauty and majesty it represents Creation in its most noble aspect.

No one who has lived amongst deodars would deny that it is the most godlike of Himalayan trees. It stands erect, dignified, and though in a strong wind it may hum and sigh and moan, it does not bend to the wind. The snow slips softly from the resilient branches. In the spring the new leaves are tender green, while in the monsoon the tiny young cones spread like blossoms in the dark green folds of the branches. The deodar thrives in the rain and enjoys the company of its own kind. Where one deodar grows, there will be others. Isolate a young tree and it will often pine away.

The great deodar forests are found along the upper reaches of the Bhagirathi valley and the Tons in Garhwal, and in Himachal and Kashmir, along the Chenab and the Jhelum, and also on the Kishanganga. I had expected to find it on the upper reaches of the Alaknanda, but could not find a single deodar along the road to Badrinath.

The average girth of the deodar varies from fifteen to twenty feet. Records show that one great deodar was 250-feet high, and more than 550 years old. The timber of these trees, which is unaffected by extremes of climate, was always highly prized for house-building. In the villages of Jaunsar Bawar, finely carved doors and windows are a feature of the timbered dwellings. Many of the quaint old bridges (some are 500 years old) over the Jhelum in Kashmir, have pillars made from whole deodar trees.

To return to my own trees, I went among them often, acknowledging their presence with a touch of my hand against their trunks—the walnut's smooth and polished, the pine's patterned and whorled; the oak's rough and gnarled, full of experience. The oak had been there the longest, and the wind had bent its upper branches and twisted a few, so that it looked shaggy and undistinguished. It is a good tree for the privacy of birds, its crooked branches spreading out with no particular effect; and sometimes the tree seems uninhabited until there is a whining sound, as of a helicopter approaching, and a party of long-tailed blue magpies stream across the forest glade.

After the monsoon, when the dark red berries had ripened on the hawthorn, this pretty tree was visited by green pigeons, the kokla-birds of Garhwal, who clambered upside-down among the fruit-laden twigs. And during winter, a white-capped redstart perched on the bare branches of the wild pear tree and whistled cheerfully. He had come to winter in the garden.

The pines grow on the next hill—the chir, the Himalayan blue pine, and the long-leaved pine—but there is a small blue pine a little way below the cottage, and sometimes I sit beneath it to listen to the wind playing softly in its branches.

Open the window at night, and there is usually something to listen to, the mellow whistle of the pygmy owlet, or the cry of a barking-deer which has scented the proximity of a panther.

Sometimes, if you are lucky, you will see the moon coming up, and two distant deodars in perfect silhouette.

Some sounds cannot be recognized. They are strange night sounds, the sounds of the trees themselves, scratching their limbs in the dark, shifting a little, flexing their fingers. Great trees of the mountains, they know me well. They know my face in the window, they see me watching them, watching them grow, listening to their secrets, bowing my head before their outstretched aims and seeking their benediction.

BETTER TO HAVE A BIRD IN A BUSH

The thing I like most about shrubs and small bushes is that they are about my size or thereabouts. I can meet them on equal terms. Most trees grow tall, they overtake us after a few years, and we find ourselves looking up to them with a certain amount of awe and deference. And so we should.

A bush, on the other hand, may have been in the ground a long time—thirty or forty years or more—while continuing to remain a bush, man-sized, and approachable. A bush may spread sideways or gain in substance, but it seldom towers over you. This means that I can be on intimate terms with it, know its qualities—of leaf, bud, flower, and fruit—and also its inhabitants, be they insects, birds, small mammals, or reptiles.

Of course, we know that bushes are ideal for binding the earth together and preventing erosion. In this respect they are just as important as trees. Every monsoon I witness landslides all about me, but I know the hillside just above my cottage is well-knit, knotted and netted, by bilberry and raspberry, wild jasmine, dog-rose and bramble, and other shrubs, vines, and creepers.

I have made a small bench in the middle of this civilized

wilderness. And sitting here, I can look down on my own roof, as well as sideways and upward, into a number of bushes, teeming with life throughout the year. This is my favourite place. No one can find me here, unless I call out and make my presence known. The buntings and sparrows, 'grown accustomed to my face' and welcoming the grain I scatter for them, flit about near my feet. One of them, bolder than the rest, alights on my shoe and proceeds to polish his beak on the leather. The sparrows are here all the year round. So are the whistling-thrushes, who live in the shadows between house and hill, sheltered by a waterwood bush, so-called because it likes cool, damp places.

Summer brings the fruit-eating birds, for, now the berries are ripe, a pair of green pigeons, rare in these parts, scramble over the branches of a hawthorn bush, delicately picking off the fruit. The raspberry bush is raided by bands of finches and greedy yellow-bottomed bulbuls. A flock of bright green parrots comes swooping down on the medlar tree, but they do not stay for long. Taking flight at my approach, they wheel above, green and gold in the sunlight, and make for the plum trees further down the road.

The kingera, a native Himalayan shrub similar to the bilberry, attracts small boys as well as birds. On their way to and from school, the boys scramble up the hillside and help themselves to the small sweet and sour berries. Then, lips stained purple, they go their merry way. The birds return.

Other inhabitants of this shrub-land include the skink, a tiny lizard-like reptile, quite harmless. It emerges from its home among stones or roots to sun itself or drink from a leaf-cup of water. I have to protect these skinks from a large prowling tabby cat who thinks the hillside and everything on it belongs to him. From my bench, I can see him move stealthily around the corner of my roof. He has his eye on the slow-moving green pigeons, I am sure. I shall have to watch out for him.

There wouldn't be much point in encouraging the birds to visit my bushes if the main beneficiary is to be that handsome, but single-minded cat!

There are flowering shrubs, too—a tangle of dog-roses, the wild yellow jasmine, a buddleia popular with honey bees, and a spreading may flower which today is covered with small saffron-winged butterflies.

The grass, straw-yellow in winter, is now green and sweet, sprinkled with buttercups and clover. I can abandon the bench and lie on the grass, studying it at close quarters while repeating Whitman's lines:

> A child said 'What is the grass?' fetching it to me with
> full hands.
> How could I answer the child? I do not know what it
> is any more than he.

I am no wiser, either, but grass is obviously a good thing, providing a home for crickets and ladybirds and other small creatures. It wouldn't be much fun, living on a planet where grass could not grow.

That cat agrees with me. He is flat on his stomach on the grass, inching closer to one of those defenceless little skinks. He has decided that a skink in hand is worth two birds in a bush. I get to my feet, and the cat runs away.

The green pigeons have also flown away. The smaller birds remain where they are; they know they are too swift for the prowler. I return to my bench and watch the finches and coppersmiths arrive and depart.

You might call my shrubbery an arrival and departure lounge for small birds, but they are also free to take up residence if they wish. Their presence adds sweetness to my life. A bush at hand is good for many a bird!

GUESTS WHO FLY IN FROM THE FOREST

When mist fills the Himalayan valleys, and heavy monsoon rain sweeps across the hills, it is natural for wild creatures to seek shelter. Any shelter is welcome in a storm—and sometimes my cottage in the forest is the most convenient refuge.

There is no doubt that I make things easier for all concerned by leaving most of my windows open—I am one of those peculiar people who like to have plenty of fresh air indoors—and if a few birds, beasts, and insects come in too, they're welcome, provided they don't make too much of a nuisance of themselves.

I must confess that I did lose patience with a bamboo beetle who blundered in the other night and fell into the water jug. I rescued him and pushed him out of the window. A few seconds later he came whirring in again, and with unerring accuracy landed with a plop in the same jug. I fished him out once more and offered him the freedom of the night. But attracted no doubt by the light and warmth of my small sitting-room, he came buzzing back, circling the room like a helicopter looking for a good place to land. Quickly I covered the water jug. He landed in a bowl of wild dahlias, and I allowed him to remain there, comfortably curled up in the hollow of a flower.

Sometimes, during the day, a bird visits me—a deep purple whistling-thrush, hopping about on long dainty legs, peering to right and left, too nervous to sing. She perches on the windowsill, looking out at the rain. She does not permit any familiarity. But if I sit quietly in my chair, she will sit quietly on her windowsill, glancing quickly at me now and then just to make sure that I'm keeping my distance. When the rain stops, she glides away, and it is only then, confident in her freedom, that she bursts into full-throated song, her broken but haunting melody echoing down the ravine.

A squirrel comes sometimes, when his home in the oak tree gets waterlogged. Apparently he is a bachelor; anyway, he lives alone. He knows me well, this squirrel, and is bold enough to climb on to the dining-table looking for tidbits which he always finds, because I leave them there deliberately. Had I met him when he was a youngster, he would have learned to eat from my hand; but I have only been here a few months. I like it this way. I am not looking for pets: these are simply guests.

Last week, as I was sitting down at my desk to write a long-deferred article, I was startled to see an emerald-green praying mantis sitting on my writing pad. He peered up at me with his protruberant glass bead eyes, and I stared down at him through my reading glasses. When I gave him a prod, he moved off in a leisurely way. Later I found him examining the binding of Whitman's *Leaves of Grass;* perhaps he had found a succulent bookworm. He disappeared for a couple of days, and then I found him on the dressing-table, preening himself before the mirror. Perhaps I am doing him an injustice in assuming that he was preening. Maybe he thought he'd met another mantis and was simply trying to make contact. Anyway, he seemed fascinated by his reflection.

Out in the garden, I spotted another mantis, perched on the jasmine bush. Its arms were raised like a boxer's. Perhaps they're a pair, I thought, and went indoors and fetched my mantis and placed him on the jasmine bush, opposite his fellow insect. He did not like what he saw—no comparison with his own image!—and made off in a huff.

My most interesting visitor comes at night, when the lights are still burning—a tiny bat who prefers to fly in at the door, should it be open, and will use the window only if there's no alternative. His object in entering the house is to snap up the moths that cluster around the lamps.

All the bats I've seen fly fairly high, keeping near the ceiling as far as possible, and only descending to ear level (my ear level) when they must; but this particular bat flies in low, like a dive bomber, and does acrobatics amongst the furniture, zooming in and out of chair legs and under tables. Once, while careening about the room in this fashion, he passed straight between my legs.

Has his radar gone wrong, I wondered, or is he just plain crazy?

I went to my shelves of *Natural History* and looked up 'bats', but could find no explanation for this erratic behaviour. As a last resort, I turned to an ancient volume, Sterndale's *Indian Mammalia* (Calcutta, 1884), and in it, to my delight, I found what I was looking for—

...a bat found near Mussoorie by Captain Hutton, on the southern range of hills at 5,500 feet; head and body, 1.4

inch; skims close to the ground, instead of flying high
as bats generally do, Habitat, Jharipani, N.W. Himalayas.

Apparently the bat was rare even in 1884.

Perhaps I've come across one of the few surviving members
of the species: Jharipani is only two miles from where I live.
And I feel rather offended that modern authorities should have
ignored this tiny bat; possibly they feel that it is already extinct.
If so, I'm pleased to have rediscovered it. I am happy that it
survives in my small corner of the woods, and I undertake to
celebrate it in prose and verse.

MY FATHER'S TREES IN DEHRA

Our trees still grow in Dehra. This is one part of the world where trees are a match for man. An old peepul may be cut down to make way for a new building; two peepul trees will sprout from the walls of the building. In Dehra the air is moist, the soil hospitable to seeds and probing roots. The valley of Dehra Dun lies between the first range of the Himalayas and the smaller but older Siwalik range. Dehra is an old town, but it was not in the reign of Rajput princes or Mogul kings that it really grew and flourished; it acquired a certain size and importance with the coming of British and Anglo-Indian settlers. The English have an affinity with trees, and in the rolling hills of Dehra they discovered a retreat which, in spite of snakes and mosquitoes, reminded them, just a little bit, of England's green and pleasant land.

The mountains to the north are austere and inhospitable; the plains to the south are flat, dry and dusty. But Dehra is green. I look out of the train window at daybreak to see the sal and shisham trees sweep by majestically, while trailing vines and great clumps of bamboo give the forest a darkness and density which add to its mystery. There are still a few tigers in these forests; only a few, and perhaps they will survive, to stalk the spotted deer and drink at forest pools.

I grew up in Dehra. My grandfather built a bungalow on the outskirts of the town at the turn of the century. The house was sold a few years after Independence. No one knows me now in Dehra, for it is over twenty years since I left the place, and my boyhood friends are scattered and lost. And although the India of *Kim* is no more, and the Grand Trunk Road is now a procession of trucks instead of a slow-moving caravan of horses and camels, India is still a country in which people are easily lost and quickly forgotten.

From the station I can take either a taxi or a snappy little scooter rickshaw (Dehra had neither before 1950), but, because I am on an unashamedly sentimental pilgrimage, I take a tonga, drawn by a lean, listless pony, and driven by a tubercular old Muslim in a shabby green waistcoat. Only two or three tongas stand outside the station. There were always twenty or thirty here in the 1940s when I came home from boarding school to be met at the station by my grandfather; but the days of the tonga are nearly over, and in many ways this is a good thing, because most tonga ponies are overworked and underfed. Its wheels squeaking from lack of oil and its seat slipping out from under me, the tonga drags me through the bazaars of Dehra. A couple of miles of this slow, funereal pace makes me impatient to use my own legs, and I dismiss the tonga when we get to the small Dilaram Bazaar.

It is a good place from which to start walking.

The Dilaram Bazaar has not changed very much. The shops are run by a new generation of bakers, barbers, and banias, but professions have not changed. The cobblers belong to the lower castes, the bakers are Muslims, the tailors are Sikhs. Boys still fly kites from the flat rooftops, and women wash clothes on the canal steps. The canal comes down from Rajpur and goes underground here, to emerge about a mile away.

I have to walk only a furlong to reach my grandfather's house. The road is lined with eucalyptus, jacaranda, and laburnum trees. In the compounds there are small groves of mangoes, litchis, and papayas. The poinsettia thrusts its scarlet leaves over garden walls. Every verandah has its bougainvillea creeper, every garden its bed of marigolds. Potted palms, those symbols of Victorian snobbery, are popular with Indian housewives. There are a few houses, but most of the bungalows were built by 'old India hands' on their retirement from the army, the police or the railways. Most of the present owners are Indian businessmen or government officials.

I am standing outside my grandfather's house. The wall has been raised, and the wicket gate has disappeared; I cannot get a clear view of the house and garden. The nameplate identifies the owner as Major General Saigal; the house has had more than one owner since my grandparents sold it in 1949.

On the other side of the road there is an orchard of litchi trees. This is not the season for fruit, and there is no one looking after the garden. By taking a little path that goes through the orchard, I reach higher ground and gain a better view of our old house.

Grandfather built the house with granite rocks taken from the foothills. It shows no sign of age. The lawn has disappeared; but the big jackfruit tree, giving shade to the side verandah, is still there. In this tree I spent my afternoons, absorbed in my Magnets, Champions and Hotspurs, while sticky mango juice trickled down my chin. (One could not eat the jackfruit unless it was cooked into a vegetable curry.) There was a hole in the bole of the tree in which I kept my pocket knife, top, catapult and any badges or buttons that could be saved from my father's RAF tunics when he came home on leave. There was also an Iron Cross, a relic of the First World War, given to me by my grandfather. I have managed to keep the Iron Cross; but what did I do with my top and catapult? Memory fails me. Possibly they are still in the hole in the jackfruit tree; I must have forgotten to collect them when we went away after my father's death. I am seized by a whimsical urge to walk in at the gate, climb into the branches of the jackfruit tree and recover my lost possessions. What would the present owner, the Major General (retired), have to say if I politely asked permission to look for a catapult left behind more than twenty years ago?

An old man is coming down the path through the litchi trees. He is not a major general but a poor street vendor. He carries a small tin trunk on his head, and walks very slowly. When he sees me, he stops and asks me if I will buy something. I can think of nothing I need, but the old man looks so tired, so very old, that I am afraid he will collapse if he moves any further along the path without resting. So I ask him to show me his wares. He cannot get the box off his head by himself, but together we manage to set it down in the shade, and the old man insists on spreading its entire contents on the grass; bangles, combs, shoelaces, safety pins, cheap stationery, buttons, pomades, elastic, and scores of other household necessities.

When I refuse buttons because there is no one to sew them on for me, he piles me with safety pins. I say no; but as he moves from one article to another, his querulous, persuasive voice slowly wears down my resistance, and I end up buying envelopes, a letter pad (pink roses on bright blue paper), a one-rupee fountain pen guaranteed to leak and several yards of elastic. I have no idea what I will do with the elastic, but the old man convinces me that I cannot live without it.

Exhausted by the effort of selling me a lot of things I obviously do not want, he closes his eyes and leans back against the trunk of a litchi tree. For a moment I feel rather nervous. Is he going to die sitting here beside me? He sinks to his haunches and puts his chin on his hands. He only wants to talk.

'I am very tired, huzoor,' he says. 'Please do not mind if I sit here for a while.'

'Rest for as long as you like,' I say. 'That's a heavy load you've been carrying.'

He comes to life at the chance of a conversation and says, 'When I was a young man, it was nothing. I could carry my box up from Rajpur to Mussoorie by the bridle path—seven steep miles! But now I find it difficult to cover the distance from the station to Dilaram Bazaar.'

'Naturally. You are quite old.'

'I am seventy, sahib.'

'You look very fit for your age.' I say this to please him; he looks frail and brittle. 'Isn't there someone to help you?' I ask.

'I had a servant boy last month, but he stole my earnings and ran off to Delhi. I wish my son was alive—he would not have permitted me to work like a mule for a living—but he was killed in the riots in 1947.'

'Have you no other relatives?'

'I have outlived them all. That is the curse of a healthy life. Your friends, your loved ones, all go before you, and in the end you are left alone. But I must go too, before long. The road to the bazaar seems to grow longer every day. The stones are harder. The sun is hotter in the summer, and the wind much colder in the winter. Even some of the trees that were there in my youth have grown old and have died. I have outlived the trees.'

He has outlived the trees. He is like an old tree himself, gnarled and twisted. I have the feeling that if he falls asleep in the orchard, he will strike root here, sending out crooked branches. I can imagine a small bent tree wearing a black waistcoat; a living scarecrow.

He closes his eyes again, but goes on talking.

'The English memsahibs would buy great quantities of elastic. Today it is ribbons and bangles for the girls, and combs for the boys. But I do not make much money. Not because I cannot walk very far. How many houses do I reach in a day? Ten, fifteen. But twenty years ago I could visit more than fifty houses. That makes a difference.'

'Have you always been here?'

'Most of my life, huzoor. I was here before they built the motor road to Mussoorie. I was here when the sahibs had their own carriages and ponies and the memsahibs their own rickshaws. I was here before there were any cinemas. I was here when the Prince of Wales came to Dehra Dun... Oh, I have been here a long time, huzoor. I was here when that house was built,' he says pointing with his chin towards my grandfather's house. 'Fifty, sixty years ago it must have been. I cannot remember exactly. What is ten years when you have lived seventy? But it was a tall, red-bearded sahib who built that house. He kept many creatures as pets. A kachwa (turtle) was one of them. And there was a python, which crawled into my box one day and gave me a terrible fright. The sahib used to keep it hanging from his shoulders, like a garland. His wife, the burra mem, always bought a lot from me—lots of elastic. And there were sons, one a teacher, another in the air force, and there were always children in the house. Beautiful children. But they went away many years ago. Everyone has gone away.'

I do not tell him that I am one of the 'beautiful children'. I doubt if he will believe me. His memories are of another age, another place, and for him there are no strong bridges into the present.

'But others have come,' I say.

'True, and that is as it should be. That is not my complaint. My complaint—should God be listening—is that I have been left behind.'

He gets slowly to his feet and stands over his shabby tin box, gazing down at it with a mix of disdain and affection. I help him to lift and balance it on the flattened cloth on his head. He does not have the energy to turn and make a salutation of any kind; but, setting his sights on the distant hills, he walks down the path with steps that are shaky and slow but still wonderfully straight.

I wonder how much longer he will live. Perhaps a year or two, perhaps a week, perhaps an hour. It will be an end of living, but it will not be death. He is too old for death; he can only sleep; he can only fall gently, like an old, crumpled brown leaf.

I leave the orchard. The bend in the road hides my grandfather's house. I reach the canal again. It emerges from under a small culvert, where ferns and maidenhair grow in the shade. The water, coming from a stream in the foothills, rushes along with a familiar sound; it does not lose its momentum until the canal has left the gently sloping streets of the town.

There are new buildings on this road, but the small police station is housed in the same old lime-washed bungalow. A couple of off-duty policemen, partly uniformed but with their pyjamas on, stroll about.

I cannot forget this little police station. Nothing very exciting ever happened in its vicinity until, in 1947, communal riots broke out in Dehra. Then, bodies were regularly fished out of the canal and dumped on a growing pile in the station compound. I was only a boy, but when I looked over the wall at that pile of corpses, there was no one who paid any attention to me. They were too busy to send me away. At the same time they knew that I was perfectly safe; while Hindus and Muslims were at each other's throats, a white boy could walk the streets in safety. No one was any longer interested in the Europeans.

The people of Dehra are not violent by nature, and the town has no history of communal discord. But when refugees from the partitioned Punjab poured into Dehra in thousands, the atmosphere became charged with tension. These refugees, many of them Sikhs, had lost their homes and livelihoods; many had seen their loved ones butchered. They were in a fierce and vengeful frame of mind. The calm, sleepy atmosphere of Dehra was shattered during two months of looting and murder. The Muslims who could get away, fled. The poorer members of the community remained in a refugee camp until the holocaust was over; then they returned to their former occupations, frightened and deeply mistrustful. The old boxman was one of them.

I cross the canal and take the road that will lead me to the riverbed. This was one of my father's favourite walks. He, too, was a walking man. Often, when he was home on leave, he would say, 'Ruskin, let's go for a walk,' and we would slip off together and walk down to the riverbed or into the sugarcane fields or across the railway lines and into the jungle.

On one of those walks (this was before Independence), I remember him saying, 'After the war is over, we'll be going to England. Would you like that?'

'I don't know,' I said. 'Can't we stay in India?'

'It won't be ours any more.'

'Has it always been ours?' I asked.

'For a long time,' he said, 'over two hundred years. But we have to give it back now.'

'Give it back to whom?' I asked. I was only nine.

'To the Indians,' said my father.

The only Indians I had known till then were my ayah and the cook and the gardener and their children, and I could not imagine them wanting to be rid of us. The only other Indian who came to the house was Dr Ghose, and it was frequently said of him that he was more English than the English. I could understand my father better when he said, 'After the war, there'll be a job for me in England. There'll be nothing for me here.'

The war had at first been a distant event; but somehow it kept coming closer. My aunt, who lived in London with her two children, was killed with them during an air raid; then my father's younger brother died of dysentery on the long walk out from Burma. Both these tragic events depressed my father. Never in good health (he had been prone to attacks of malaria), he looked more worn and wasted every time he came home. His personal life was far from being happy, as he and my mother had separated, she to marry again. I think he looked forward a great deal to the days he spent with me; far more than I could have realized at the time. I was someone to come back to; someone for whom things could be planned; someone who could learn from him.

Dehra suited him. He was always happy when he was among trees, and this happiness communicated itself to me. I felt like drawing close to him. I remember sitting beside him on the verandah steps when I noticed the tendril of a creeping vine that was trailing near my feet. As we sat there, doing nothing in particular—in the best gardens, time has no meaning—I found that the tendril was moving almost imperceptibly away from me and towards my father. Twenty minutes later it had crossed the verandah steps and was touching his feet. This, in India, is the sweetest of salutations.

There is probably a scientific explanation for the plant's behaviour—something to do with the light and warmth on the verandah steps—but I like to think that its movements were motivated simply by an affection for my father. Sometimes, when I sat alone beneath a tree, I felt a little lonely or lost. As soon as my father rejoined me, the atmosphere lightened, the tree itself became more friendly.

Most of the fruit trees round the house were planted by father; but he was not content with planting trees in the garden. On rainy days we would walk beyond the riverbed, armed with cuttings and saplings, and then we would amble through the jungle, planting flowering shrubs between the sal and shisham trees.

'But no one ever comes here,' I protested the first time. 'Who is going to see them?'

'Some day,' he said, 'someone may come this way... If people keep cutting trees, instead of planting them, there'll soon be no forests left at all, and the world will be just one vast desert.' The prospect of a world without trees became a sort of nightmare for me (and one reason why I shall never want to live on the treeless moon), and I assisted my father in his tree planting with great enthusiasm.

'One day the trees will move again,' he said. 'They've been standing still for thousands of years. There was a time when they could walk about like people, but someone cast a spell on them and rooted them to one place. But they're always trying to move—see how they reach out with their arms!'

We found an island, a small rocky island in the middle of a dry riverbed. It was one of those riverbeds, so common in the foothills, which are completely dry in the summer but flooded during the monsoon rains. The rains had just begun, and the stream could still be crossed on foot, when we set out with a number of tamarind, laburnum, and coral tree saplings and cuttings. We spent the day planting them on the island, then ate our lunch there, in the shelter of a wild plum.

My father went away soon after that tree planting. Three months later, in Calcutta, he died.

I was sent to boarding school. My grandparents sold the house and left Dehra. After school, I went to England. The years passed, my grandparents died, and when I returned to India I was the only member of the family in the country.

And now I am in Dehra again, on the road to the riverbed. The houses with their trim gardens are soon behind me, and I am walking through fields of flowering mustard, which make a carpet of yellow blossom stretching away towards the jungle and the foothills.

The riverbed is dry at this time of the year. A herd of skinny cattle graze on the short brown grass at the edge of the jungle. The sal trees have been thinned out. Could our trees have survived? Will our island be there, or has some flash flood during a heavy monsoon washed it away completely?

As I look across the dry watercourse, my eye is caught by the spectacular red plumes of the coral blossom. In contrast with the dry, rocky riverbed, the little island is a green oasis. I walk across to the trees and notice that a number of parrots have come to live in them. A koel challenges me with a rising *who-are-you, who-are you.*

But the trees seem to know me. They whisper among themselves and beckon me nearer. And looking around, I find that other trees and wild plants and grasses have sprung up under the protection of the trees we planted.

They have multiplied. They are moving. In this small forgotten corner of the world, my father's dreams are coming true, and the trees are moving again.

A WILDERNESS IN NEW DELHI

If you are determined, you can find a wilderness close to you, no matter where you live. In 1959, I was living on the outskirts of a greater, further New Delhi. The influx of refugees from the Punjab after Partition had led to many new colonies springing up on the outskirts of the capital, and at the time, the furthest of these was Rajouri Garden. Needless to say, there were no gardens. The treeless colony was buffeted by hot, dusty winds from Haryana and Rajasthan. The houses were built on one side of Najafgarh Road. On the other side, as yet uncolonized, were extensive fields of wheat and other crops still belonging to the original inhabitants. In an attempt to escape the city life that constantly oppressed me, I would walk across the main road and into the fields, finding old wells, irrigation channels, camels and buffaloes, and sighting birds and small creatures that no longer dwelt in the city life, which led to my taking a greater interest in the natural world. Up to that time, I had taken it all for granted. The notebook I kept at the time lies before me now, and my first entry describes the blue jays or rollers that were much a feature of those remaining open spaces. At rest, the bird is fairly nondescript, but when it takes flight it reveals the glorious bright blue wings and the tail, banded with a lighter blue. It sits motionless, but the large dark eyes are constantly watching the ground in every direction. A grasshopper or cricket has only to make a brief appearance, and the blue jay will launch itself straight at its prey. In spring and early summer the 'roller' lives up to its other name. It indulges in love flights, in which it rises and falls in the air with harsh grating screams—a real rock 'n' roller!

Some way down the Najafgarh Road was a large village pond and beside it a magnificent banyan tree. We have no place for banyan trees today, they need so much space in which to spread their limbs and live comfortably. Cut away its aerial roots and the great tree topples over—usually to make way for a spacious apartment building. That was the first banyan tree I got to know well. It had about a hundred pillars supporting the boughs, and above them there was a great leafy crown like a pillared hall. It has been said that whole armies could shelter in the shade of an old banyan. And probably at one time they did. I saw another sort of army visit the banyan by the village pond when it was in fruit. Parakeets, mynas, rosy pastors, crested bulbuls without crests, barbets and many other birds crowded the tree in order to feast noisily on big scarlet figs. Even further down the Najafgarh Road was a large jheel, famous for its fishing. I wonder if any part of the jheel still exists, or if it got filled in and became a part of greater Delhi. One could rest in the shade of a small babul or keekar tree and watch the kingfisher skim over the water, making just a slight splash as it dived and came up with small glistening fish. Our common Indian kingfisher is a beautiful little bird with a brilliant blue back, a white throat and orange underparts. I would spot one perched on an overhanging bush or rock, and wait to see it plunge like an arrow into the water and return to its perch to devour the catch. It came over the water in a flash of gleaming blue, shrilling its loud 'tit-tit-tit'. The kingfisher is the subject of a number of legends, and the one I remember best, recounted by Romain Rolland, tells us that it was originally a plain grey bird that acquired its resplendent colours by flying straight towards the sun when Noah let it out of the ark. Its upper plumage took the colour of the sky above, while the lower was scorched a deep russet by the rays of the setting sun. Summer and winter, I scorned the dust and the traffic, and walked all over Delhi, in search of quiet spots with some shade, a few birds, flower, and fruit. I spent many afternoons lying on the grass near India Gate and eating jamuns. I liked the sour tang of the jamun fruit, which was best eaten with a little salt. And I liked the deep purple colour of the fruit. Jamuns were one of the nicer things about Delhi.

MOUNTAINS IN MY BLOOD

It was while I was living in England, in the jostle and drizzle of London, that I remembered the Himalayas at their most vivid. I had grown up amongst those great blue and brown mountains; they had nourished my blood; and though I was separated from them by thousands of miles of ocean, plain and desert, I could not rid them from my system. It is always the same with mountains. Once you have lived with them for any length of time, you belong to them. There is no escape.

And so, in London in March, the fog became a mountain mist, and boom of traffic became the boom of the Ganges emerging from the foothills.

I remembered a little mountain path which led my restless feet into a cool, sweet forest of oak and rhododendron, and then on to the windswept crest of a naked hilltop. The hill was called Clouds End. It commanded a view of the plains on one side, and of the snow peaks on the other. Little silver rivers twisted across the valley below, where the rice—fields formed a patchwork of emerald green. And on the hill itself, the wind made a *hoo-hoo-hoo* in the branches of the tall deodars where it found itself trapped.

During the rains, clouds enveloped the valley but left the hill alone, an island in the sky. Wild sorrel grew amongst the rocks, and there were many flowers—convolvulus, clover, wild begonia, dandelion—sprinkling the hillside.

On a spur of the hill stood the ruins of an old brewery. The roof had long since disappeared, and the rain had beaten the stone floors smooth and yellow. Some enterprising Englishman had spent a lifetime here making beer for his thirsty compatriots in the plains. Now, moss and ferns and maidenhair grew from the walls. In a hollow beneath a flight of worn stone steps, a wild cat had made its home. It was a beautiful grey creature, black-striped, with pale green eyes. Sometimes it watched me from the steps or the wall, but it never came near.

No one lived on the hill, except occasionally a coal-burner in a temporary grass-thatched hut. But villagers used the path, grazing their sheep and cattle on the grassy slopes. Each cow or sheep had a bell suspended from its neck, to let the shepherd-boy know of its whereabouts. The boy could then lie in the sun and eat wild strawberries without tear of losing his animals.

I remembered some of the shepherd boys and girls.

There was a boy who played a flute. Its rough, sweet, straightforward notes travelled clearly across the mountain air. He would greet me with a nod of his head, without taking the flute from his lips. There was a girl who was nearly always cutting grass for fodder. She wore heavy bangles on her feet, and long silver earrings. She did not speak much either, but she always had a wide grin on her face when she met me on the path. She used to sing to herself, or to the sheep, to the grass, or to the sickle in her hand.

And there was a boy who carried milk into town (a distance of about five miles), who would often fall into step with me, to hold a long conversation. He had never been away from the hills, or in a large city. He had never been on a train. I told him about the cities, and he told me about his village; how they make bread from maize, how fish were to be caught in the mountain streams, how the bears came to steal his father's pumpkins. Whenever the pumpkins were ripe, he told me, the bears would come and carry them off.

These things I remembered—these, and the smell of pine needles, the silver of oak-leaves and the red of maple, the call of the Himalayan cuckoo, and the mist, like a wet face-cloth, pressing against the hills.

Odd, how some little incident, some snatch of conversation, comes back to one again and again, in the most unlikely places. Standing in the aisle of a crowded tube train on a Monday morning, my nose tucked into the back page of someone else's newspaper, I suddenly had a vision of a bear making off with a ripe pumpkin.

A bear and a pumpkin—and there, between Goodge Street and Tottenham Court Road stations, all the smells and sounds of the Himalayas came rushing back to me.

◆

Lost all my money

I've lost all my money,
And I'm on my way home;
Home to the hills and a field of rocks.
Nothing in the city but a sickness of the soul,
Nothing to earn but sorrow...
I've lost all my money

And I'm on my way home,
With nothing to buy my way home...
I've lost all my money
And I can't bribe the guard,
So help me, O Lord,
On my way home...

HAROLD: OUR HORNBILL

Harold's mother, like all good hornbills, was the most careful of wives. His father was the most easy-going of husbands. In January, long before the flame tree flowered, Harold's father took his wife into a great hole high in the tree trunk, where his father and his father's father had taken their brides at the same time every year.

In this weather-beaten hollow, generation upon generation of hornbills had been raised. Harold's mother, like those before her, was enclosed within the hole by a sturdy wall of earth, sticks, and dung.

Harold's father left a small hole in the centre of this wall to enable him to communicate with his wife whenever he felt like a chat. Walled up in her uncomfortable room, Harold's mother was a prisoner for over two months. During this period an egg was laid, and Harold was born.

In his naked boyhood Harold was no beauty. His most promising feature was his flaming red bill, matching the blossoms of the flame tree which was now ablaze, heralding the summer. He had a stomach that could never be filled, despite the best efforts of his parents who brought him pieces of jackfruit and berries from the banyan tree.

As he grew bigger, the room became more cramped, and one day his mother burst through the wall, spread out her wings and sailed over the tree-tops. Her husband was glad to see her about. He played with her, expressing his delight with deep gurgles and throaty chuckles. Then they repaired the wall of the nursery, so that Harold would not fall out.

Harold was quite happy in his cell, and felt no urge for freedom. He was putting on weight and a philosophy of his own. Then something happened to change the course of his life.

One afternoon he was awakened from his siesta by a loud thumping on the wall, a sound quite different from that made by his parents. Soon the wall gave way, and there was something large and yellow and furry staring at him—not his parents' bills, but the hungry eyes of a civet cat.

Before Harold could be seized, his parents flew at the cat, both roaring lustily and striking out with their great bills. In the ensuing melee, Harold tumbled out of his nest and landed on our garden path.

Before the cat or any predator could get to him, Grandfather picked him up and took him to the sanctuary of the verandah.

Harold had lost some wing feathers and did not look as though he would be able to survive on his own, so we made an enclosure for him on our front verandah. Grandfather and I took over the duties of his parents.

Harold had a simple outlook, and once he had got over some early attacks of nerves, he began to welcome the approach of people. Grandfather and I meant the arrival of food and he greeted us with craning neck, quivering open bill, and a loud, croaking, 'Ka-ka-kaee!'

Fruit, insect or animal food, and green leaves were all

welcome. We soon dispensed with the enclosure, but Harold made no effort to go away; he had difficulty flying. In fact, he asserted his tenancy rights, at least as far as the verandah was concerned.

One afternoon a verandah tea party was suddenly and alarmingly convulsed by a flash of black and white and noisy flapping. And behold, the last and only loaf of bread had been seized and carried off to his perch near the ceiling.

Harold was not beautiful by Hollywood standards. He had it a small body and a large head. But he was good-natured and friendly, and he remained on good terms with most members of the household during his lifetime of twelve years.

Harold's best friends were those who fed him, and he was willing even to share his food with us, sometimes trying to feed me with his great beak.

While I turned down his offers of beetles and similar delicacies, I did occasionally share a banana with him. Eating was a serious business for Harold, and if there was any delay at mealtimes he would summon me with raucous barks and vigorous bangs of his bill on the woodwork of the kitchen window.

Having no family, profession or religion, Harold gave much time and thought to his personal appearance. He carried a rouge pot on his person and used it very skilfully as an item of his morning toilet.

This rouge pot was a small gland situated above the roots of his tail feathers; it produced a rich yellow fluid. Harold would dip into his rouge pot from time to time and then rub the colour over his feathers and the back of his neck. It would come off on my hands whenever I touched him.

Harold would toy with anything bright or glittering, often

swallowing it afterwards.

He loved bananas and dates and balls of boiled rice. I would throw him the rice balls, and he would catch them in his beak, toss them in the air, and let them drop into his open mouth.

He perfected this trick of catching things, and in time I taught him to catch a tennis ball thrown with some force from a distance of fifteen yards. He would have made a great baseball catcher or an excellent slip fielder. On one occasion he seized a rupee coin from me (a week's pocket money in those days) and swallowed it neatly.

Only once did he really misbehave. That was when he removed a lighted cigar from the hand of an American cousin who was visiting us. Harold swallowed the cigar. It was a moving experience for Harold, and an unnerving one for our guest.

Although Harold never seemed to drink any water, he loved the rain. We always knew when it was going to rain because Harold would start chuckling to himself about an hour before the first raindrops fell.

This used to irritate Aunt Ruby. She was always being caught in the rain. Harold would be chuckling when she left the house. And when she returned, drenched to the skin, he would be in fits of laughter.

As storm clouds would gather, and gusts of wind would shake the banana trees, Harold would get very excited, and his chuckle would change to an eerie whistle.

'Wheee...wheee,' he would scream, and then, as the first drops of rain hit the verandah steps, and the scent of the fresh earth passed through the house, he would start roaring with pleasure.

The wind would carry the rain into the verandah, and Harold would spread out his wings and dance, tumbling about like a circus clown. My grandparents and I would come out on the verandah and share his happiness.

Many years later, I still miss Harold's raucous bark and the banging of his great bill. If there is a heaven for good hornbills, I sincerely hope he is getting all the summer showers he could wish for, and plenty of tennis balls to catch.

WHEN GUAVAS ARE RIPE

Guava trees are easy to climb. And guavas are good to eat. So it's little wonder that an orchard of guava trees is a popular place with boys and girls.

Just across the road from Ranji's house, on the other side of a low wall, was a large guava orchard. The monsoon rains were almost over. It was a warm humid day in September, and the guavas were ripening, turning from green to gold—no longer hard, but growing soft and sweet and juicy.

The schools were closed because of a religious festival. Ranji's father was at work. Ranji's mother was enjoying an afternoon siesta on a cot in the backyard. His grandmother was busy teaching her pet parrot to recite a prayer.

'I feel like getting into those guava trees,' said Ranji to himself. 'It's months since I climbed a tree.'

He was soon across the road and over the wall and into the trees. He chose a tree that grew in the middle of the orchard, where it was unlikely that he would be disturbed, then he climbed swiftly into its branches. A cluster of guavas swung just above him. He reached up for one of them, but to his surprise he found himself clutching a small bare foot which had suddenly been thrust through the foliage.

Having caught the foot, Ranji did not let go. Instead he pulled hard on it. There was a squeal and someone came toppling down on him. Ranji found himself clutching at arms and legs. Together they crashed through a couple of branches and landed with a thud on the soft ground beneath the tree.

Ranji and the intruder struggled fiercely. They rolled about on the grass. Ranji tried a judo hold—without any success. Then he saw that his opponent was a girl. It was his friend and neighbour, Koki.

'It's you!' he gasped.

'It's me,' said Koki. 'And what are *you* doing here?'

'Get your knee out of my stomach and I'll tell you.'

When he recovered his breath, he said, 'I just felt like climbing a tree.'

'So did I.'

He stared at her. There was guava juice at the corners of her mouth and on her chin.

'Are the guavas good?' he asked.

'Quite sweet, in this tree,' said Koki. 'You find another tree for yourself, Ranji. There must be thirty or forty trees to choose from.'

'And all going to waste,' said Ranji. 'Look, some of the guavas have been spoilt by the birds.'

'Nobody wants them, it seems.'

Koki climbed back into her tree, and Ranji obligingly walked a little further and climbed another tree. After a few polite exchanges they fell silent, their attention given over entirely to the eating of guavas.

'I've eaten five,' said Koki after some time.

'You'd better stop.'

'You're only saying that because you've just started.'

'Well, three's enough for me.'

'I'm getting a tummy ache, I think.'

'I warned you. Come on, I'll take you home. We can come back tomorrow. There are still lots of guavas left. Hundreds!'

'I don't think I want to eat any more,' said Koki.

◆

She felt better the next day—so well, in fact, that Ranji found her leaning on the gate, waiting for him to join her. She was accompanied by her small brother, Teju, who was only six and very mischievous.

'How are you feeling today?' asked Ranji.

'Hungry,' said Koki.

'Why did you bring your brother?'

'He wants to start climbing trees.'

Soon they were in the orchard. Ranji and Koki helped Teju into the branches of one of the smaller trees and then made for other trees, disturbing a party of parrots who flew in circles around the orchard, screaming their protests.

Two boys and a girl talking to each other from three different trees can make quite a lot of noise, and it wasn't only the birds who were disturbed. Though they did not know it, the orchard belonged to a wealthy property dealer and he employed a watchman, whose duty was to keep away birds, children, monkeys, flying foxes, and other fruit-eating pests. But on a hot, sultry afternoon Gopal, the watchman, could not resist taking a nap. He was stretched out under a shady jackfruit tree, snoring so loudly that the flies that had been buzzing around him felt that a storm was brewing and kept their distance.

He woke to the sound of voices raised high in glee. Sitting

up, he brushed a ladybird from his long moustache, then seized his lathi.

'Who's there?' he shouted, struggling to his feet.

There was a sudden silence in the trees.

'Who's there?' he called again.

No answer.

'I must have been dreaming,' he muttered, and was preparing to lie down and take another nap when Teju, who had been watching him, burst into laughter.

'Ho!' shouted the watchman, coming to life again.

'Thieves! I'll settle you!' And he began striding towards the centre of the orchard, boasting all the time of his physical prowess. 'I am not afraid of thieves, bandits, or wild beasts! I'll have you know that I was once the wrestling champion of an entire district of Dehra. Come on out and fight me if you dare!'

'Run!' hissed Koki, scrambling down her tree.

'Run!' shouted Ranji, as though it were a cricket match.

Teju was so startled by the sudden activity that he tumbled out of his tree and began crying, and Ranji and Koki had to go to his aid.

The sight of an enormous ex-wrestler bearing down on them was enough to make Teju stop crying and get to his feet. Then all three were fleeing across the grove, the watchman a little way behind them, waving his lathi and shouting at the top of his voice. Although he was an ex-wrestler (or perhaps because of it) he could not run very fast, and was still huffing and puffing some twenty metres behind them when they climbed up and over the wall. He could not climb walls either.

They ran off in different directions before returning home.

◆

The next day, Ranji met Koki and Teju at the far end of the road.

'Is he there?' asked Koki.

'I haven't seen him. But he must be around somewhere.'

'Maybe he's gone for his lunch. We'll just walk past and take a quick look.'

The three of them strolled casually down the road. Koki said the gardens were looking very pretty. Teju gazed admiringly at a boy flying a kite from a rooftop. Ranji kept one eye on the road and one eye on the orchard wall. A squirrel ran along the top of the wall; the parrots were back in the guava trees.

They moved closer to the wall. Ranji leaned casually against it and Koki began to pick little daisies growing at the edge of the road. Teju, unable to hide his curiosity, pulled himself up on the wall and looked over. At the same time Gopal, the watchman, who had been hiding behind the wall waiting for them, stood up slowly and glared fiercely at Teju.

Teju gulped, but he did not flinch. He was looking straight into the watchman's red angry eyes.

'And what can I do for you?' said Gopal.

'I was just looking,' said Teju.

'At what?'

'At the view.'

Gopal was a little baffled. They looked just like the children he'd chased away yesterday, but he couldn't be sure. They didn't *look* guilty. But did children ever look guilty?

'There's a better view from the other side of the road,' he said gruffly. 'Now be off!'

'What lovely guavas,' said Koki, smiling sweetly. There weren't many people who could resist that smile!

'True,' said Ranji, with the air of one who was an expert on guavas and all things good to eat. 'They are just the right size and colour. I don't think I've seen better. But they'll be spoilt by the birds if you don't gather them soon.'

'It's none of your business,' said the watchman.

'Just look at his muscles,' said Teju, trying a different approach. 'He's really strong!'

Gopal looked pleased for once. He was proud of his former prowess, even though he was now rather flabby around the waist.

'You look like a wrestler,' said Ranji.

'I *am* a wrestler,' said Gopal.

'I told you so,' said Koki. 'What else could he be?'

'I'm a retired wrestler,' said Gopal.

'You don't look retired,' said Teju, fast learning that flattery can get you almost anywhere.

Gopal swelled with pride; such admiration hadn't come his way for a long time. To Koki he looked like a bullfrog swelling up, but she thought it better not to say so.

'Do you want to see my muscles?' he asked.

'Yes, yes!' they cried. 'Do show us!'

Gopal peeled off his shirt and thumped his chest. It sounded like a drum. They were really impressed. Then he bent his elbow and his biceps stood up like cricket balls.

'You can touch them,' he said generously.

Teju poked a finger into Gopal's biceps.

'Mister Universe!' he exclaimed.

Gopal glowed all over. He liked these children. How intelligent they were! Not everyone had the sense to appreciate his strength, his manliness, his magnificent physique!

'Climb over the wall and join me,' he said. 'Come sit on the grass and I'll tell you about the time when I was a wrestling champion.'

Over the wall they came, and sat politely on the grass. Gopal told them about some of his exploits, how he had vanquished a world-famous wrestler in five seconds flat, and how he had saved a carload of travellers from drowning by single-handedly dragging their car out of a river. They listened patiently. Then Teju mentioned that he was feeling hungry.

'Hungry?' said Gopal. 'Why didn't you tell me before? I'll bring you some guavas, that's all there is to eat here. I know which tree has the best ones. And they're all going to rot if no one eats them—no one's buying the crop this year, the owner's price is too high!'

Gopal hurried off and soon returned with a basket full of guavas.

'Help yourselves,' he said. 'But don't eat too many, you'll get sick.'

So they munched guavas and listened to Gopal tell them about the time he was waylaid by three bandits and how he threw them all into the village pond.

'Will you come again tomorrow?' asked Gopal eagerly, when the guavas were finished and the children got up to leave. 'Come tomorrow and I'll tell you another story.'

'We'll come tomorrow,' said Teju, looking at all the guava trees laden with fruit.

Somehow it seemed very important to Gopal that they should come again. It was lonely in the orchard. Koki sensed this, and said, 'We like your stories.'

'They are good stories,' said Ranji, even if they were not entirely true, he thought...

They climbed over the wall and waved goodbye to Gopal.

◆

They came again the next day.

And even when the guava season was over and Gopal had nothing to offer them but his stories, they went to see him because by that time they had grown to like him.

THE PROSPECT OF FLOWERS

Fern Hill, The Oaks, Hunter's Lodge, The Parsonage, The Pines, Dumbarnie, Mackinnon's Hall and Windermere. These are the names of some of the old houses that still stand on the outskirts of one of the smaller Indian hill stations. Most of them have fallen into decay and ruin. They are very old, of course—built over a hundred years ago by Britishers who sought relief from the searing heat of the plains. Today's visitors to the hill stations prefer to live near the markets and cinemas, and many of the old houses, set amidst oak and maple and deodar, are inhabited by wildcats, bandicoots, owls, goats and the occasional charcoal burner or mule driver.

But amongst these neglected mansions stands a neat, whitewashed cottage called Mulberry Lodge. And in it, up to a short time ago, lived an elderly English spinster named Miss Mackenzie.

In years Miss Mackenzie was more than 'elderly', being well over eighty. But no one would have guessed it. She was clean, sprightly, and wore old-fashioned but well-preserved dresses. Once a week, she walked the two miles to town to buy butter and jam and soap and sometimes a small bottle of eau de cologne.

She had lived in the hill station since she had been a girl in her teens, and that had been before the First World War. Though she had never married, she had experienced a few love affairs and was far from being the typical frustrated spinster of fiction. Her parents had been dead thirty years; her brother and sister were also dead. She had no relatives in India, and she lived on a small pension of forty rupees a month and the gift parcels that were sent out to her from New Zealand by a friend of her youth.

Like other lonely old people, she kept a pet—a large black cat with bright yellow eyes. In her small garden she grew dahlias, chrysanthemums, gladioli and a few rare orchids. She knew a great deal about plants and about wild flowers, trees, birds and insects. She had never made a serious study of these things, but having lived with them for so many years had developed an intimacy with all that grew and flourished around her.

She had few visitors. Occasionally, the padre from the local church called on her, and once a month the postman came with a letter from New Zealand or her pension papers. The milkman called every second day with a litre of milk for the lady and her cat. And sometimes she received a couple of eggs free, for the egg-seller remembered a time when Miss Mackenzie, in her earlier prosperity, had bought eggs from him in large quantities. He was a sentimental man. He remembered her as a ravishing beauty in her twenties when he had gazed at her in round-eyed, nine-year-old wonder and consternation.

Now it was September and the rains were nearly over, and Miss Mackenzie's chrysanthemums were coming into their own. She hoped the coming winter wouldn't be too severe because she found it increasingly difficult to bear the cold.

One day, as she was pottering about in her garden, she saw a schoolboy plucking wild flowers on the slope about the cottage.

'Who's that?' she called. 'What are you up to, young man?'

The boy was alarmed and tried to dash up the hillside, but he slipped on pine needles and came slithering down the slope on to Miss Mackenzie's nasturtium bed.

When he found there was no escape, he gave a bright disarming smile and said, 'Good morning, miss.'

He belonged to the local English-medium school and wore a bright red blazer and a red-and-black striped tie. Like most polite Indian schoolboys, he called every woman 'miss'.

'Good morning,' said Miss Mackenzie severely. 'Would you mind moving out of my flower bed?'

The boy stepped gingerly over the nasturtiums and looked up at Miss Mackenzie with dimpled cheeks and appealing eyes. It was impossible to be angry with him.

'You're trespassing,' said Miss Mackenzie.

'Yes, miss.'

'And you ought to be in school at this hour.'

'Yes, miss.'

'Then what are you doing here?'

'Picking flowers, miss.' And he held up a bunch of ferns and wild flowers.

'Oh.' Miss Mackenzie was disarmed. It was a long time since she had seen a boy taking an interest in flowers, and, what was more, playing truant from school in order to gather them.

'Do you like flowers?' she asked.

'Yes, miss. I'm going to be a botan—a botantist?'

'You mean a botanist.'

'Yes, miss.'

'Well, that's unusual. Most boys at your age want to be pilots or soldiers or perhaps engineers. But you want to be a botanist. Well, well. There's still hope for the world, I see. And do you know the names of these flowers?'

'This is a *bukhilo* flower,' he said, showing her a small golden flower. 'That's a Pahari name. It means puja or prayer. The flower is offered during prayers. But I don't know what this is…'

He held out a pale pink flower with a soft, heart-shaped leaf.

'It's a wild begonia,' said Miss Mackenzie. 'And that purple stuff is salvia, but it isn't wild. It's a plant that escaped from my garden. Don't you have any books on flowers?'

'No, miss.'

'All right, come in and I'll show you a book.'

She led the boy into a small front room, which was crowded with furniture and books and vases and jam jars, and offered him a chair. He sat awkwardly on its edge. The black cat immediately leapt on to his knees, and settled down on them, purring loudly.

'What's your name?' asked Miss Mackenzie, as she rummaged through her books.

'Anil, miss.'

'And where do you live?'

'When school closes, I go to Delhi. My father has a business.'

'Oh, and what's that?'

'Bulbs, miss.'

'Flower bulbs?'

'No, electric bulbs.'

'Electric bulbs! You might send me a few, when you get home. Mine are always fusing, and they're so expensive, like everything else these days. Ah, here we are!' She pulled a heavy volume down from the shelf and laid it on the table. '*Flora Himaliensis,* published in 1892, and probably the only copy in India. This is a very valuable book, Anil. No other naturalist has recorded so many wild Himalayan flowers. And let me tell you this, there are many flowers and plants which are still unknown to the fancy botanists who spend all their time with microscopes instead of in the mountains. But perhaps, *you'll* do something about that, one day.'

'Yes, miss.'

They went through the book together, and Miss Mackenzie pointed out many flowers that grew in and around the hill station, while the boy made notes of their names and seasons. She lit a stove, and put the kettle on for tea. And then the old English lady and the small Indian boy sat side by side over cups of hot sweet tea, absorbed in a book on wild flowers.

'May I come again?' asked Anil, when finally he rose to go.

'If you like,' said Miss Mackenzie. 'But not during school hours. You mustn't miss your classes.'

After that, Anil visited Miss Mackenzie about once a week, and nearly always brought a wild flower for her to identify. She found herself looking forward to the boy's visits—and sometimes, when more than a week passed and he didn't come, she was disappointed and lonely and would grumble at the black cat.

Anil reminded her of her brother, when the latter had been a boy. There was no physical resemblance. Andrew had been fair-haired and blue-eyed. But it was Anil's eagerness, his alert, bright look and the way he stood—legs apart, hands on hips, a picture of confidence—that reminded her of the boy who had shared her own youth in these same hills.

And why did Anil come to see her so often?

Partly because she knew about wild flowers, and he really did want to become a botanist. And partly because she smelt of freshly baked bread, and that was a smell his own grandmother had possessed. And partly because she was lonely and sometimes a boy of twelve can sense loneliness better than an adult. And partly because he was a little different from other children.

By the middle of October, when there was only a fortnight left for the school to close, the first snow had fallen on the distant mountains. One peak stood high above the rest, a white pinnacle against the azure-blue sky. When the sun set, this peak turned from orange to gold to pink to red.

'How high is that mountain?' asked Anil.

'It must be over 12,000 feet,' said Miss Mackenzie. 'About thirty miles from here, as the crow flies. I always wanted to go there, but there was no proper road. At that height, there'll be flowers that you don't get here—the blue gentian and the purple columbine, the anemone, and the edelweiss.'

'I'll go there one day,' said Anil.

'I'm sure you will, if you really want to.'

The day before his school closed, Anil came to say goodbye to Miss Mackenzie.

'I don't suppose you'll be able to find many wild flowers in Delhi,' she said. 'But have a good holiday.'

'Thank you, miss.'

As he was about to leave, Miss Mackenzie, on an impulse, thrust the *Flora Himaliensis* into his hands.

'You keep it,' she said. 'It's a present for you.'

'But I'll be back next year, and I'll be able to look at it then. It's so valuable.'

'I know it's valuable and that's why I've given it to you. Otherwise it will only fall into the hands of the junk dealers.'

'But, miss...'

'Don't argue. Besides, I may not be here next year.'

'Are you going away?'

'I'm not sure. I may go to England.'

She had no intention of going to England; she had not seen the country since she was a child, and she knew she would not fit in with the life of post-war Britain. Her home was in these hills, among the oaks and maples and deodars. It was lonely, but at her age it would be lonely anywhere.

The boy tucked the book under his arm, straightened his tie, stood stiffly to attention and said, 'Goodbye, Miss Mackenzie.'

It was the first time he had spoken her name.

Winter set in early and strong winds brought rain and sleet, and soon there were no flowers in the garden or on the hillside. The cat stayed indoors, curled up at the foot of Miss Mackenzie's bed.

Miss Mackenzie wrapped herself up in all her old shawls and mufflers, but still she felt the cold. Her fingers grew so stiff that she took almost an hour to open a can of baked beans. And then it snowed and for several days the milkman did not come. The postman arrived with her pension papers, but she felt too tired to take them up to town to the bank.

She spent most of the time in bed. It was the warmest place. She kept a hot-water bottle at her back, and the cat kept her feet warm. She lay in bed, dreaming of the spring and summer months. In three months' time the primroses would be out, and with the coming of spring the boy would return.

One night the hot-water bottle burst and the bedding was soaked through. As there was no sun for several days, the blanket remained damp. Miss Mackenzie caught a chill and had to keep to her cold, uncomfortable bed. She knew she had a fever but there was no thermometer with which to take her temperature. She had difficulty in breathing.

A strong wind sprang up one night, and the window flew open and kept banging all night. Miss Mackenzie was too weak to get up and close it, and the wind swept the rain and sleet into the room. The cat crept into the bed and snuggled close to its mistress's warm body. But towards morning that body had lost its warmth and the cat left the bed and started scratching about on the floor.

As a shaft of sunlight streamed through the open window, the milkman arrived. He poured some milk into the cat's saucer on the doorstep, and the cat leapt down from the windowsill and made for the milk.

The milkman called a greeting to Miss Mackenzie, but received no answer. Her window was open and he had always known her to be up before sunrise. So he put his head in at the window and called again. But Miss Mackenzie did not answer. She had gone away to the mountain where the blue gentian and purple columbine grew.

TO THE RIVER

It was raining when we woke, and the mountains were hidden by a heavy mist. We delayed our departure, playing football on the verandah with one of the pumpkins that had fallen off the roof. At noon the rain stopped and the sun shone through the clouds. As the mist lifted, we saw the snow range, the great peaks of Nanda Kot and Trisul stepping into the sky.

'It's different up here,' said Kamal. 'I feel a different person.'

'That's the altitude,' I said. 'As we go higher, we'll get lighter in the head.'

'Anil is light in the head already,' said Kamal. 'I hope the altitude isn't too much for him.'

'If you two are going to be witty,' said Anil, 'I shall go off with Bisnu, and you'll have to find the way yourselves.'

Bisnu grinned at each of us in turn to show that he wasn't taking sides; and after a breakfast of boiled eggs, we set off on our trek to the next bungalow.

Rain had made the ground slippery, and we were soon ankle-deep in slush. Our next bungalow lay in a narrow valley, on the banks of the rushing Pindar river, which twisted its way through the mountains. We were not sure how far we had to go, but nobody seemed in a hurry. On an impulse, I decided to hurry on ahead of the others. I wanted to be waiting for them at the river.

The path dropped steeply, then rose and went round a big mountain. I met a woodcutter and asked him how far it was to the river. He was a short, stocky man, with gnarled hands and a weathered face.

'Seven miles,' he said. 'Are you alone?'

'No, the others are following but I cannot wait for them. If you meet them, tell them I'll be waiting at the river.'

The path descended steeply now, and I had to run a little. It was a dizzy, winding path. The hillside was covered with lush green ferns, and in the trees, unseen birds sang loudly. Soon I was in the valley, and the path straightened out. A girl was coming from the opposite direction. She held a long curved knife, with which she had been cutting grass and fodder. There were rings in her nose and ears, and her arms were covered with heavy bangles. The bangles made music when she moved her hands—it was as though her hands spoke a language of their own.

'How far is it to the river?' I asked.

The girl had probably never been near the river, or she may have been thinking of another one, because she replied, 'Twenty miles', without any hesitation.

I laughed, and ran down the path. A parrot screeched suddenly, flew low over my head—a flash of blue and green—and took the course of the path, while I followed its dipping flight, until the path rose and the bird disappeared into the trees.

A trickle of water came from the hillside, and I stopped to drink. The water was cold and sharp and very refreshing. I had walked alone for nearly an hour. Presently I saw a boy ahead of me, driving a few goals along the path.

'How far is it to the river?' I asked, when I caught up with him.

The boy said, 'Oh, not far, just round the next hill.'

As I was hungry, I produced some dry bread from my pocket and breaking it in two, offered half to the boy. We sat on the grassy hillside and ate in silence. Then we walked on together and began talking and talking. I did not notice the smarting of my feet and the distance I had covered. But after some time the boy had to diverge along another path, and I was once more on my own.

I missed the village boy. I looked up and down the path, but I could see no one, no sign of Anil and Kamal and Bisnu, and the river was not in sight either. I began to feel discouraged. But I couldn't turn back; I was determined to be at the river before the others.

And so I walked on, along the muddy path, past terraced fields and small stone houses, until there were no more fields and houses, only forest and sun and silence.

The silence was impressive and a little frightening. It was different from the silence of a room or an empty street. Nor was there any movement, except for the bending of grass beneath my feet, and the circling of a hawk high above the fir trees.

And then, as I rounded a sharp bend, the silence broke into sound.

The sound of the river.

Far down in the valley, the river tumbled over itself in its impatience to reach the plains. I began to run, slipped and stumbled, but continued running.

And the water was blue and white and wonderful.

When Anil, Kamal, and Bisnu arrived, the four of us bravely

decided to bathe in the little river. The late afternoon sun was still warm but the water—so clear and inviting—proved to be ice-cold. Only twenty miles upstream the river emerged as a little trickle from the glacier; and in its swift descent down the mountain slopes it did not give the sun a chance to penetrate its waters. But we were determined to bathe, to wash away the dust and sweat of our two day's trudging, and we leapt about in the shallows like startled porpoises, slapping water on each other and gasping with the shock of each immersion. Bisnu, more accustomed to mountain streams than ourselves, ventured across in an attempt to catch an otter, but wasn't fast enough. Then we were on the springy grass, wrestling each other in order to get warm.

The bungalow stood on an edge just above the river, and the sound of the water rushing down the mountainside could be heard at all times. The sound of the birds which we had grown used to, was drowned by the sound of the water, but the birds themselves could be seen, many-coloured, standing out splendidly against the dark green forest foliage—the red-crowned jay, the paradise fly-catcher, the purple whistling-thrush, and others we could not recognize.

Higher up the mountain, above some terraced land where oats and barley were grown, stood a smaller cluster of huts. This, we were told by the watchman, was the last village on the way to the glacier. It was, in fact, one of the last villages in India, because if we crossed the difficult passes beyond the glacier, we would find ourselves in Tibet. We told the watchman we would be quite satisfied if we reached the glacier.

Then Anil made the mistake of mentioning the Abominable Snowman, of whom we had been reading in the papers. The people of Nepal believe in the existence of the Snowman, and our watchman was a Nepali.

'Yes, I have seen the Yeti,' he told us. 'A great shaggy flat-footed creature. In the winter, when it snows heavily, he passes by the bungalow at night. I have seen his tracks the next morning.'

'Does he come this way in the summer?' I asked anxiously. We were sitting before another of Bisnu's fires, drinking tea with condensed milk, and trying to get through a black, sticky sweet which the watchman had produced from his tin trunk.

'The Yeti doesn't come here in the summer,' said the old man. 'But I have seen the Lidini sometimes. You have to be careful of her.'

'What is a Lidini?' asked Kamal.

'Ah!' said the watchman mysteriously. 'You have heard of the Abominable Snowman, no doubt, but few have heard of the Abominable Snowwoman! And yet she is far more dangerous of the two!'

'What is she like?' asked Anil, and we all craned forward.

'She is of the same height as the Yeti—about seven feet when her back is straight—and her hair is much longer. She has very long teeth and nails. Her feet face inward, but she can run very fast, especially downhill. If you see a Lidini, and she chases you, always run away in an uphill direction. She tires quickly because of her feet. But when running downhill she has no trouble at all, and you have to be very fast to escape her!'

'Well, we're all good runners,' said Anil with a nervous laugh. 'But it's just a fairy story, I don't believe a word of it.'

'But you must believe fairy stories,' I said, remembering a performance of Peter Pan in London, when those in the audience who believed in fairies were asked to clap their hands in order to save Tinker Bell's life. 'Even if they aren't true,' I added, deciding there was a world of difference between Tinker

Bell and the Abominable Snowwoman.

'Well, I don't believe there's a Snowman or a Snowwoman!' declared Anil.

The watchman was most offended and refused to tell us anything about the Sagpa and Sagpani; but Bisnu knew about them, and later, when we were in bed, he told us that they were similar to Snowwomen but much smaller. Their favourite past-time was sleeping, and they became very annoyed if anyone woke them, and became ferocious, and did not give one much time to start running uphill. The Sagpa and Sagpani sometimes kidnapped small children, and taking them to their cave, would look after the children very carefully, feeding them on fruits, honey, rice, and earthworms.

'When the Sagpa isn't looking,' he said, 'you can throw the earthworms over your shoulder.'

WHEN YOU CAN'T CLIMB TREES ANYMORE

He stood on the grass verge by the side of the road and looked over the garden wall at the old house. It hadn't changed much. There's little anyone can do to alter a house built with solid blocks of granite brought from the riverbed. But there was a new outhouse, and there were fewer trees. He was pleased to see that the jack-fruit tree still stood at the side of the building, casting its shade on the wall. He remembered his grandmother saying: 'A blessing rests on the house where falls the shadow of a tree.' And so the present owners must also be the recipients of the tree's blessings.

At the spot where he stood there had once been a turnstile, and as a boy he would swing on it, going round and round until he was quite dizzy. Now the turnstile had gone, the opening walled up. Tall hollyhocks grew on the other side of the wall.

'What are you looking at?'

It was a disembodied voice at first. Moments later a girl stood framed between dark red hollyhocks, staring at the man it was difficult to guess her age; she might have been twelve or she might have been sixteen: slim and dark, with lovely eyes and long black hair.

'I'm looking at the house,' he said.

'Why? Do you want to buy it?'

'Is it your house?'

'It's my father's.'

'And what does your father do?'

'He's only a colonel.'

'*Only* a colonel?'

'Well, he should have been a brigadier by now.'

The man burst out laughing.

'It's not funny,' she said. 'Even mummy says he should have been a brigadier.'

It was on the tip of his tongue to make a witty remark ('Perhaps that's why he's still a colonel'), but he did not want to give offence. They stood on either side of the wall, appraising each other.

'Well,' she said finally. 'If you don't want to buy the house, what are you looking at?'

'I used to live here once.'

'Oh.'

'Twenty-five years ago. When I was a boy. And then again, when I was a young man...until my grandmother died, and then we sold the house and went away.'

She was silent for a while, taking in this information. Then she said. 'And you'd like to buy it back now, but you don't have the money?' He did not look very prosperous.

'No, I wasn't thinking of buying it back. I wanted to see it again, that's all. How long have you lived here?'

'Only three years.' She smiled. She'd been eating a melon, and there was still juice at the corners of her mouth. 'Would you like to come in—and look—once more?'

'Wouldn't your parents mind?'

'They've gone to the club. They won't mind. I'm allowed to bring my friends home.'

'Even adult friends?'

'How old are you?'

'Oh, just middle-aged, but feeling young today.' And to prove it he decided he'd climb over the wall instead of going round by the gate. He got up on the wall all right, but had to rest there, breathing heavily. 'Middle-aged man on the flying trapeze,' he muttered to himself.

'Let me help you,' she said, and gave him her hand.

He slithered down into a flower-bed, shattering the stem of a hollyhock.

As they walked across the grass he noticed a stone bench under a mango tree. It was the bench on which his grandmother used to sit, when she tired of pruning rose bushes and bougainvillaea.

'Let's sit here,' he said. 'I don't want to go inside.'

She sat beside him on the bench. It was March, and the mango tree was in bloom. A sweet, heavy fragrance drenched the garden

They were silent for some time. The man closed his eyes and remembered other times—the music of a piano, the chiming of a grandfather clock, the constant twitter of budgerigars on the verandah, his grandfather cranking up the old car...

'I used to climb the jackfruit tree,' he said, opening his eyes. 'I didn't like the jackfruit, though. Do you?'

'It's all right in pickles.'

'I suppose so... The tree was easy to climb, I spent a lot of time in it.'

'Do you want to climb it again? My parents won't mind.'

'No, I don't think so. Not after climbing the wall! Let's just sit here for a few minutes and talk. I mentioned the jackfruit tree because it was my favourite place. Do you see that thick branch stretching out over the roof? Half-way along it there's a small hollow in which I used to keep some of my treasures.'

'What kind of treasures?'

'Oh, nothing very valuable. Marbles I'd won. A book I wasn't supposed to read. A few old coins I'd collected. Things came and went. There was my Grandfather's medal, well not his exactly, because he was British and the Iron Cross was a German decoration, awarded for bravery during the War—that's the first World War—when Grandfather fought in France. He got it from a German soldier.'

'Dead or alive?'

'Pardon?' Oh, you mean the German. I never asked. Dead, I suppose. Or perhaps he was a prisoner. I never asked Grandfather. Isn't that strange?'

'And the Iron Cross? Do you still have it?'

'No,' he said, looking her in the eye. 'I left it in the jackfruit tree.

'You left it in the tree!'

'Yes, I was so busy at the time—packing, and saying goodbye to friends, and thinking about the ship I was going to sail on— that I just forgot all about it.'

She was silent, considering, her finger on her lips, her gaze fixed on the jackfruit tree.

Then, quietly, she said, 'It may still be there. In the hollow of the branch.'

'Yes,' he said. 'After twenty-five years, it may still be there. Unless someone else found it.'

'Would you like to take a look?'

'I can't climb trees any more.

'I can! I'll go and see. You just sit here and wait for me.'

She sprang up and ran across the grass, swift and sweet of limb. Soon she was in the jackfruit tree, crawling along the projecting branch. A warm wind brought little eddies of dust along the road. Summer was in the air. Ah, if only he could learn to climb trees again!

'I've found something!' she cried.

And now, barefoot, she runs breathlessly towards him, in her outstretched hand a rusty old medal.

He takes it from her and turns it over on his palm.

'Is it the Iron Cross?' she asks eagerly.

'Yes, this is it.'

'Now I know why you came. You wanted to see if it was still in the tree.'

'I don't know, I'm not really sure why I came. But you can keep the Cross. You found it, after all.'

'No, you keep it. It's yours.'

'But it might have remained in the tree for a hundred years if you hadn't gone to look for it.'

'Only because you came back—'

'On the right day, at the right time, and with the right person.' Getting up, he squeezed the hard rusty medal into her soft palm. 'No, it wasn't the Cross I came for. It was my lost youth.'

She understood this, even though her own youth still lay ahead of her, she understood it, not as an adult, but with the wisdom of the child that was still part of her. She walked with him to the gate and stood there gazing after him as he walked away. Where the road turned, he glanced back and waved to her. Then he quickened his step and moved briskly towards the bus stop. There was a spring in his step. Something cried aloud in his heart.

MOTHER HILL

It is hard to realize that I've been here all these years—twenty-five summers, winters and Himalayan springs. When I look back to the time of my first coming here, it does seem like yesterday.

That probably sums it all up. Time passes, and yet it doesn't pass; people come and go, the mountains remain. Mountains are permanent things. They are stubborn, they refuse to move. You can blast holes out of them for their mineral wealth, strip them of their trees and foliage, or dam their streams and divert their currents. You can make tunnels and roads and bridges; but no matter how hard they try, humans cannot actually get rid of the mountains. That's what I like about them; they are here to stay.

I like to think that I have become a part of these mountains, this particular range, and that by living here for so long, I am able to claim a relationship with the trees, wild flowers, and even the rocks that are an integral part of it.

Yesterday at twilight, when I passed beneath a canopy of oak leaves, I felt that I was a part of the forest. I put out my hand and touched the bark of an old tree, and as I turned away, its leaves brushed against my face as if to acknowledge me.

One day, I thought, if we trouble these great creatures too much, and hack away at them and destroy their young, they will simply uproot themselves and march away, whole forests on the move, over the next range and next, far from the haunts of man. I have seen many forests and green places dwindle and disappear. Now there is an outcry. It is suddenly fashionable to be an environmentalist. That's all right. Perhaps, it is not too late to save the little that is left.

By and large, writers have to stay in the plains to make a living. Hill people have their work cut out trying to wrest a livelihood from their thin, calcinated soil. And as for mountaineers, they climb their peaks and move on in search of other peaks.

But to me, as a writer, mountains have been kind. They were kind from the beginning, when I left a job in Delhi and rented a small cottage on the outskirts of the hill station. Today, most hill stations are rich men's playgrounds, but years ago they were places where people of modest means would live quite cheaply. There were few cars and everyone walked about.

The cottage was on the edge of an oak and maple forest and I spent eight or nine years in it, most of them happy, writing stories, essays, poems and books for children. I think this had something to do with Prem's children. He and his wife had taken on the job of looking after the house and all practical matters (I remain helpless with fuses, clogged cisterns, leaking gas cylinders, ruptured water pipes, tin roofs that blow away when there is a storm, and the do-it-yourself world of small-town India).

Naturally, I grew attached to them and became a part of the family, an adopted grandfather. For Rakesh, I wrote a story about a cherry tree that had difficulty in growing up. For Mukesh, who liked upheavals, I wrote a story about an earthquake and put him in it, and for Dolly I wrote rhymes.

'Who goes to the Hills, goes to his Mother', wrote Kipling, and he seldom wrote truer words. For living in the hills was like living in the bosom of a strong, sometimes proud, but always a comforting mother. And every time I went away, the homecoming would be tender and precious. It became increasingly difficult for me to go away.

It has not always been happiness and light though. There were times when money ran out. Editorial doors sometimes close; but when one door closes another has, for me, almost immediately, miraculously opened.

When you have received love from people and the freedom that only mountains can give, then you have come very near the borders of Heaven.

SONG OF THE WHISTLING THRUSH

I had been in the hills for a few days when I heard the song of the Himalayan whistling thrush. I did not see the bird that day. It kept to the deep shadows of the ravine below the old stone cottage. I was sitting at the window, gazing out at the new leaves on the walnut and wild pear trees. All was still; the wind was at peace with itself, the mountains brooded massively under the darkening sky. Then, emerging from the depths of the forest like a dark, sweet secret, came the indescribably beautiful call of the whistling thrush.

It is a song that never fails to thrill me. The bird starts with a hesitant schoolboy whistle, as though trying out the melody; then, confident of the time, it bursts into full song, a crescendo of sweet notes and variations that ring clearly across the hillside. Then suddenly the song breaks off, right in the middle of a cadenza, and the enchanted listener is left wondering what happened to the bird to make it stop so suddenly. Nothing really, because a few moments later the song is taken up again.

At first the bird was heard but never seen. Then one day I found the whistling thrush perched on the garden fence. He was a deep, glistening purple, his shoulders flecked with white; he had sturdy black legs and a strong yellow beak; rather a dapper fellow, who could have looked well in a top hat dancing with Fred Astaire. When he saw me coming down the path he uttered a sharp kree-ee—unexpectedly harsh when one remembered his singing—and flew away into the shadowed ravine.

But as the months passed he grew used to my presence and became less shy. One of my rainwater pipes had blocked, resulting in an overflow and a small permanent puddle under the stone steps. This became the thrush's favourite bathing place. On sultry summer afternoons, while I was taking a siesta upstairs, I would hear the bird flapping about in the rainwater pool. A little later, refreshed and sunning himself on the tin roof, he would treat me to a little concert, performed, I cannot help feeling, especially for my benefit.

It was Prakash, the man who brought my milk, who told me the story of the whistling thrush, or the Irstura or Kaljit, as the hillmen called the bird. According to legend, the god Krishna fell asleep near a mountain stream, and while he slept, a small boy made off with his famous flute. On waking up and finding his flute gone, Krishna was so angry that he changed the culprit into a bird; but the boy had played on the flute and learned some of Krishna's wonderful music, and even as a bird he continued, in his disrespectful fashion, to whistle the music of the gods, only stopping now and then (as the whistling thrush does) when he couldn't remember the right time.

It wasn't long before my thrush was joined by a female, who was exactly like him (in fact, I have never been able to tell one from the other). The pair did not sing duets, like Nelson Eddy and Jeanette MacDonald,[1] but preferred to give solo

---

[1] Famous singers from my boyhood.

performances, waiting for each other to finish before bursting into song. When, as sometimes happened, they started off together, the effect was not so pleasing to my human ear.

These were love calls, no doubt, and it wasn't long before the pair were making forays into the rocky ledges of the ravine, looking for a suitable nesting site; but a couple of years were to pass before I saw any of their young.

After almost two years in the hills, I came to realize that these were birds 'for all seasons'. They were liveliest in midsummer, but even in the depths of winter, with snow lying on the ground, they would suddenly start singing as they flitted from pine to oak to naked chestnut.

As I write, there is a strong wind rushing through the trees and bustling in the chimney, while distant thunder threatens a summer storm. Undismayed, the whistling thrushes are calling to each other as they roam the wind-threshed forest.

At other times I have heard them clearly above the sound of rushing water. And sometimes they leave the vicinity of the cottage and fly down to the stream, half a mile away, sending me little messages on the wind. Down there, they are busy snapping up snails and insects, the chief items on their menu.

Whistling thrushes usually nest on rocky ledges, near water, but my overtures of friendship may have given my visitors other ideas. Recently I was away from Mussoorie for about a fortnight. When I returned I was about to open the window when I noticed a large bundle of ferns, lichen, grass, mud and moss balanced outside on the window ledge. Peering through the glass, I was able to recognise this untidy basket as a nest. Could such tidy birds make such untidy nests? Indeed they could, because they arrived and proved their ownership a few minutes later.

Well, of course that meant I couldn't open the window

any more—the nest would have gone over the ledge if I had. Fortunately, the room has another window and I kept this one open to let in sunshine, fresh air, and the music of birds, cicadas, and the ever welcome postman.

And now, three pink, freckled eggs lie in the cup of moss that forms the nursery in this jumble of a nest. The parent birds, both male and female, come and go, bustling about very efficiently, fully prepared for the great day that's coming about a fortnight hence.

One small thought occurs to me. The song of one thrush was bright and cheerful. The song of two thrushes was loud and joyful. But won't a choir of five whistling thrushes be a little too much for a solitary writer trying to concentrate at his typewriter? Will I have to make a choice between writing or listening to the birds? Will I have to hand the cottage to other denizens of the forest? Well, we shall have to wait and see. If readers do not hear from me again, they will know who to blame!

THE CORAL TREE

The night had been hot, the rain frequent, and I slept on the verandah instead of in the house. I was in my twenties and I had begun to earn a living and felt I had certain responsibilities. In a short while a tonga would take me to a railway station, and from there a train would take me to Bombay, and then a ship would take me to England. There would be work, interviews, a job, a different kind of life; so many things that this small bungalow of my grandfather's would be remembered fitfully, in rare moments of reflection.

When I awoke on the verandah I saw a grey morning, smelt the rain on the red earth, and remembered that I had to go away. A girl was standing on the verandah porch, looking at me very seriously. When I saw her, I sat up in bed with a start.

She was a small, dark girl, her eyes big and black, her pigtails tied up in a bright red ribbon; and she was fresh and clean like the rain and the red earth.

She stood looking at me, and she was very serious.

'Hello,' I said, smiling, trying to put her at ease.

But the girl was businesslike. She acknowledged my greeting with a brief nod.

'Can I do anything for you?' I asked, stretching my limbs. 'Do you stay near here?'

She nodded again.

'With your parents?'

With great assurance she said, 'Yes. But I can stay on my own.'

'You're like me,' I said, and for a while I forgot about being an old man of twenty. 'I like to do things on my own. I'm going away today.'

'Oh,' she said, a little breathlessly.

'Would you care to go to England?'

'I want to go everywhere,' she said, 'to America and Africa and Japan and Honolulu.'

'Maybe you will,' I said. 'I'm going everywhere, and no one can stop me... But what is it you want? What did you come for?'

'I want some flowers but I can't reach them.' She waved her hand towards the garden. 'That tree, see?'

The coral tree stood in front of the house surrounded by pools of water and broken, fallen blossoms. The branches of the tree were thick with the scarlet, pea-shaped flowers.

'All right,' I said. 'Just let me get ready.'

The tree was easy to climb, and I made myself comfortable on one of the lower branches, smiling down at the serious upturned face of the girl.

'I'll throw them down to you,' I said.

I bent a branch but the wood was young and green, and I had to twist it several times before it snapped.

'I'm not sure that I ought to do this,' I said, as I dropped the flowering branch to the girl.

'Don't worry,' she said.

'Well, if you're ready to speak up for me—'

'Don't worry.'

I felt a sudden nostalgic longing for childhood and an urge to remain behind in my grandfather's house with its tangled memories and ghosts of yesteryear. But I was the only one left, and what could I do except climb coral and jackfruit trees?

'Have you many friends?' I asked.

'Oh, yes.'

'Who is the best?'

'The cook. He lets me stay in the kitchen, which is more interesting than the house. And I like to watch him cooking. And he gives me things to eat, and tells me stories...'

'And who is your second best friend?'

She inclined her head to one side, and thought very hard. 'I'll make you the second best,' she said.

I sprinkled coral blossoms over her head. 'That's very kind of you. I'm happy to be your second best.'

A tonga bell sounded at the gate, and I looked out from the tree and said, 'It's come for me. I have to go now.'

I climbed down.

'Will you help me with my suitcases?' I asked, as we walked together towards the verandah. 'There is no one here to help me. I am the last to go. Not because I want to go, but because I have to.'

I sat down on the cot and packed a few last things in a suitcase. All the doors of the house were locked. On my way to the station I would leave the keys with the caretaker. I had already given instructions to an agent to try and sell the house. There was nothing more to be done.

We walked in silence to the waiting tonga, thinking and wondering about each other.

'Take me to the station,' I said to the tonga driver.

The girl stood at the side of the path, on the damp red earth, gazing at me.

'Thank you,' I Mid. 'I hope I shall see you again.'

'I'll see you in London,' she said, 'or America or Japan. I want to go everywhere.'

'I'm sure you will,' I said. 'And perhaps I'll come back and we'll meet again in this garden. That would be nice, wouldn't it?'

She nodded and smiled. We knew it was an important moment.

The tonga driver spoke to his pony, and the carriage set off down the gravel path, rattling a little. The girl and I waved to each other.

In the girl's hand was a sprig of coral blossom. As she waved, the blossoms fell apart and danced lightly in the breeze.

'Goodbye!' I called.

'Goodbye!' called the girl.

The ribbon had come loose from her pigtail and lay on the ground with the coral blossoms.

'I'm going everywhere,' I said to myself, 'and no one can stop me'.

And she was fresh and clean like the rain and the red earth.

IN SEARCH OF SWEET PEAS

If someone were to ask me to choose between writing an essay on the Taj Mahal or on the last rose of the summer, I'd take the rose—even if it was down to its last petal. Beautiful, cold, white marble leaves me—well, just a little cold… Roses are warm and fragrant, and almost every flower I know, wild or cultivated, has its own unique quality, whether it be subtle fragrance or arresting colour or liveliness of design. Unfortunately, winter has come to the Himalayas, and the hillsides are now brown and dry, the only colour being that of the red sorrel growing from the limestone rocks. Even my small garden looks rather forlorn, with the year's last dark-eyed nesturtium looking every bit like the Lone Ranger surveying the surrounding wilderness from his saddle. The marigolds have dried in the sun and tomorrow I will gather the seeds. The beanstalk that grew rampant during the monsoon is now down to a few yellow leaves and empty bean-pods.

'This won't do,' I told myself the other day. 'I must have flowers.' Prem, who had been to the valley town of Dehra the previous week, had made me even more restless, because he had spoken of masses of sweet peas in full bloom in the garden of one of the town's public schools. Down in the plains, winter is the best time for gardens, and I remembered my grandmother's house in Dehra, with its long rows of hollyhocks, neatly-stalked sweet peas and beds ablaze with red salvia and antirrhinum. Neither grandmother nor the house are there anymore. But surely there are other beautiful gardens, I mused, and maybe I could visit the school where Prem had seen the sweet peas. It was a long time since I had enjoyed their delicate fragrance.

So I took the bus down the hill, and throughout the twohour journey, I dozed and dreamt of gardens—cottage gardens in the English countryside, tropical gardens in Florida, Mughal gardens in Kashmir, the Hanging Gardens of Babylon—what had they been like, I wondered.

And then we were in Dehra, and I got down from the bus and walked down the dusty, busy road to the school Prem had told me about.

It was encircled by a high wall, and, tip-toeing, I could see playing fields and extensive school buildings and, in the far distance, a dollop of colour which may have been a garden. Prem's eyesight was obviously better than mine.

Anyway, I made my way to a wrought iron gate that would have done justice to a medieval fortress, and found it chained and locked. On the other side stood a tough looking guard, with a rifle.

'May I enter?' I asked.

'Sorry, sir, today is holiday. No school today.'

'I don't want to attend classes, I want to see the sweet peas.'

'Kitchen is on the other side of the ground.'

'Not green peas. Sweet peas. I'm looking for the garden.'

'I am guard here.'

'Garden.'

'No garden, only guard.'

I tried telling him that I was an old boy of the school and that I was visiting the town after a long interval. This was true up to a point, because I had once been admitted to this very school, and after one day's attendance had insisted on going back to my old school. The guard was unimpressed. And perhaps it was poetic justice that the gates were barred to me now.

Disconsolate, I strolled down the main road, past a garage, a cinema, a row of cheap eating houses and tea shops. Behind the shops there seemed to be a park of sorts, but you couldn't see much of it from the road because of the buildings, the press of the people, and the passing trucks and buses. But I found the entrance, unbarred this time, and struggled through patches of overgrown shrubbery until, like Alice after finding the golden key to the little door in the wall, I looked upon a lovely little garden.

There were no sweet peas, true, and the small fountain was dry. But around it, filling a large circular bed, were masses of bright yellow Californian poppies!

They stood out like sunshine after the rain, and my heart leapt as Wordsworth's must have done when he saw his daffodils. I found myself oblivious to the sounds of the bazaar and the road, just as the people outside seemed oblivious to this little garden. It was as though it had been waiting here all the time. Waiting for me to come by and discover it.

I am very fortunate. Something like this is always happening to me. As grandmother often said, 'When one door closes, another door opens.' And while one gate had been closed upon the sweet peas, another had opened on Californian poppies.

◆

Trees make you feel younger. And the older the tree, the younger you feel.

Whenever I pass beneath the old tamarind tree standing sentinel in the middle of Dehra's busiest street crossing, the years fall away and I am a boy again, sitting on the railing that circled the tree, while across the road, Granny ascended the steps of the Allahabad Bank, where she kept her savings.

The bank is still there, but the surroundings have changed, the traffic and the noise is far greater than it used to be, and I wouldn't dream of sauntering across the road as casually as I would have done in those days. The press of people is greater too, reflecting the tenfold increase in population that has taken place in this and other north Indian towns during the last forty years. But the old tamarind has managed to survive it all. As long as it stands, as long as its roots still cling to Dehra's rich soil, I shall feel confident that my own roots are well embedded in this old valley town.

There was a time when almost every Indian village had its spreading banyan tree, in whose generous shade, schoolteachers conducted open-air classes, village elders met to discuss matters of moment, and itinerant merchants spread out their ware. Squirrels, birds of many kinds, flying-foxes, and giant beetles, are just some, of the many inhabitants of this gentle giant. Ancient banyan trees are still to be found in some parts of the country; but as villages grow into towns, and towns into cities, the banyan is gradually disappearing. It needs a lot of space for its aerial roots to travel and support it, and space is now at a premium.

If you can't find a banyan, a mango grove is a wonderful place for a quiet stroll or an afternoon siesta. In traditional paintings, it is often the haunt of young lovers. But if the mangoes are ripening, there is not much privacy in a mango grove. Parrots, crows, monkeys and small boys are all attempting to evade the watchman who uses an empty gasoline tin as a drum to frighten away these intruders.

The mango and the banyan don't grow above the foothills, and here in the mountains, the more familiar trees are the Himalayan oaks, horse-chestnuts, rhododendrons, pines and deodars. The deodar (from the Sanskrit dev-dar, meaning Tree of God) resembles the cedar of Lebanon, and can grow to a great height in a few hundred years. There are a number of giant deodars on the outskirts of Mussoorie, where I live, and they make the town seem quite young. Mussoorie is only 160 years old. The deodars are at least twice that age.

These are gregarious trees—they like being among their own kind—and a forest of deodars is an imposing sight. When a mountain is covered with them, they look like an army on the march: the only kind of army one would like to see marching over the mountains! Although the world has already lost over half its forest cover, these sturdy giants look as though they are going to be around a long time, given half a chance.

The world's oldest trees, a species of pine, grow in California and have been known to live up to five thousand years. Is that why Californians look so young?

The oldest tree I have seen is an ancient mulberry growing at Joshimath, a small temple town in the Himalayas. It is known as the Kalp-Vriksha or Immortal Tree. The Hindu sage, Sankaracharya, is said to have meditated beneath it in the sixteenth century. These ancient sages always found a suitable tree beneath which they could meditate. The Buddha favoured a banyan tree, while Hindu ascetics are still to be found sitting cross-legged beneath peepal trees. Peepals are just right in summer, because the slender heart-shaped leaves catch the slightest breeze and send cool currents down to the thinker below.

Personally, I prefer contemplation to meditation. I am happy to stand back from the great mulberry and study its awesome proportions. Not a tall tree, but it has an immense girth—my three-room apartment in Mussoorie would have fitted quite snugly into it. A small temple beside the tree looked very tiny indeed, and the children playing among its protruding roots could have been kittens.

As I said, I'm not one for meditating beneath trees, but that's really because something always happens to me when I try. I don't know how the great sages managed, but I find it difficult to concentrate when a Rhesus monkey comes up to me and stares me in the face. Or when a horse-chestnut bounces off my head. Or when a cloud of pollen slides off the branch of a deodar and down the back of my shirt. Or when a woodpecker starts hammering away a few feet up the trunk from where I sit. I expect the great ones were immune to all this arboreal activity. I'm just a nature-lover, easily distracted by the caterpillar crawling up my leg.

And so I am happy to stand back and admire the 'good, green-hatted people', as a visitor from another planet described the trees in a story by R.L. Stevenson. Especially the old trees. They have seen a lot of odd humans coming and going, and they know I'm just a seventy-year-old boy without any pretensions to being a sage.